TOTAL MELTDOWN

HELLFIRE BOOK #7

ELLE JAMES

TWISTED PAGE INC

TOTAL MELTDOWN

HELLFIRE BOOK #7

New York Times & USA Today
Bestselling Author

ELLE JAMES

AUTHOR'S NOTE

Enjoy these other books in the HELLFIRE Series
by Elle James

Hellfire Series

Hellfire, Texas (#1)
Justice Burning (#2)
Smoldering Desire (#3)
Hellfire in High Heels (#4)
Playing With Fire (#5)
Up in Flames (#6)
Total Meltdown (#7)

Visit ellejames.com for more titles and release dates
For hot cowboys, visit her alter ego Myla Jackson at
mylajackson.com
and join Elle James and Myla Jackson's Newsletter at
Newsletter

This book is dedicated to my best buddy ever, Chewy. Short for Chewbacca, this little spitfire of a Yorkie melted my heart from the first day I saw him. He's been my shadow, my muse and my best friend. As he grows old, I love him even more. I know someday he will not be with me anymore, and I'll be heartbroken. But I'll have all the good memories of how funny, perky and devoted he was.

Love you, Chewy!

Escape with...

Elle James

aka Myla Jackson

CHAPTER 1

"So, Lily, where are you going this summer?" Lola Engel stood beside Lily Grayson in the playground of the elementary school in Hellfire, Texas.

Lily sighed. "My job with the Pattersons fell through at the last minute. Mia Patterson's mother had a heart attack. They didn't feel like they could leave for their scheduled summer in Corfu, Greece this year."

Lola shook her head. "Wow, I'd give my favorite Salvatore Ferragamo Gancini sandals to go to Greece."

Lily chuckled. "That's saying a lot. I know how attached you are to them."

"After the fire, I wrote the company and had them find me the same pair and ship them overnight. I think I paid nearly half the insurance settlement for that pair. I just couldn't sleep knowing I might not wear them again." Lola gave a side-eye glance to Lily. "Don't judge. I could have worse vices."

Lily held up her hands. "I'm not judging. I love those shoes, too." Her friend had a shoe fetish she didn't really understand, but she loved the woman despite her quirks, or maybe because of her quirks.

"So, you're not going to Greece." Lola shrugged. "I could use a part time helper at the shop for the summer, if you need the money and want to stay busy."

"I don't really need the money. You know me, living at the family ranch, I don't have to pay rent and I pitch in some for utilities, but I really don't have many expenses. I could just spend my money and take a trip somewhere."

"Or not and stay here and keep me company at the shop." Lola raised her eyebrows. "You could teach me some more of that Krav Maga stuff, so I can kick some poor schmuck's booty who tries to hit on me at the Ugly Stick Saloon."

Lily shook her head. "You have Daniel now. No one's going to poach on his territory.

Lola smiled. "I do have Daniel." She hugged herself. "He's so deliciously yummy and attentive in the—"

Lily shot a frown her direction. "Shh. Remember where you are." She tipped her head toward the playground where the children climbed on the bars, played on the slide and swings or jumped rope.

Lola cover her mouth. "Sorry. I'm here to help you, not have the parents of your little angels filing complaints about what their child learned on the last day of school." She stared at the children. "Although, they'll learn it all sooner or later. They'll be teenagers before we all know it."

"Let it be later." Lily glanced at her watch. "Thanks for helping with Field Day. The last day of school is always a challenge to keep them from climbing the walls. They have so much energy and are so eager to get out and do summer activities." Lily smiled. "I'll miss them. This class was so special."

"Do you have a favorite student? You know, teacher's pet?" Lola asked.

Lily shook her head. "Can't do that. You have to love them all equally." Although, there was one child she would miss the most.

Roberto Delossantos ran toward her with a wild-flower gripped in his fist. "Miss Grayson, look what I found."

Lily squatted down beside the little boy who was small for his age, but so precious with his light brown curls and green eyes. His smile always brightened her day. She held out her hand. "What have you got?"

"A flower for you." He held out the offering with a huge grin.

"Thank you, Robbie. It's beautiful."

"Do you know what it's called?" Robbie asked. Throughout the spring, Robbie had brought her every wildflower the playground had to offer so that she could tell him what it was called. She'd had to brush up on her flowers to answer him.

Lily examined the bright orange flower with the equally bright yellow tips on each petal. "That's called a Fire Wheel or Indian Blanket."

He beamed up at her. "It's pretty, like you, Miss Grayson." His smile slipped. "Do we have to stay home for the summer?"

Lily pulled the little guy into a hug. "Oh, sweetie, we don't have school during the summer."

He wrapped his arms around her neck and held on tight. "But I want to stay here with you."

Lily untangled his arms from around her and held him at arm's length so that she could look into his eyes. "I won't be here, Robbie. The school will be closed. Besides, the summer is meant for you to spend time with your family."

A small frown drew his dark brows together. "But my father will be in Costa Rica."

Lily frowned. She knew Robbie's mother wasn't in the picture but wasn't sure why. Just that she wasn't around. At all. "You have your little sister. She'll be happy to have you at home. Who will you be staying with?"

"Rosa," Robbie said. "She keeps us during the summer."

Rosa was the woman who dropped him off and

picked him up at school every day. She was listed on his emergency data card, along with his father. But Rosa was an older woman, probably in her mid-fifties.

He gazed at his shoes. "I don't want to stay with Rosa."

"Have you talked to your father?" Lily asked.

The little boy shook his head then lifted it, his eyes wide.

Lily wondered if Robbie's father was abusive. He rarely came to the school. Only twice during the school year had he come to collect Robbie, and only because Rosa had been on vacation or sick. Lily's heart hurt for the little boy.

"I'm sorry, Robbie. I wish I could be with you during the summer, but I'm sure you'll have fun anyway."

He hugged her again, burying his face against her neck. "When I grow up, I'm going to marry you, Miss Grayson."

She hugged him back. "When you grow up, you'll change your mind." Again, she set him to arm's length. "Now, it's a beautiful day. Go play."

The little boy ran off to climb on the monkey bars.

"I believe you have an admirer," Lola murmured beside her.

Lily sighed. "It really is hard when they leave. They're like my own children. I've spent more time with them throughout the school year than they have with their parents."

"What's with little Robbie's parents? Are they never there for him?"

"I think his mother is out of the picture completely. Robbie never talks about her, and she's not the one who picks him up at the end of the day."

"What about his father?"

"He's a wealthy rancher who also has business interests in Costa Rica. Apparently, he goes there often. It's too bad he doesn't take his children with him. They need to spend more time with him."

The bell rang, and the children lined up in front of each of their teachers.

Lily led the front of the line back to the classroom, while Lola brought up the rear, keeping the stragglers from straying. Though they were noisier than usual, Lily didn't have the heart to chastise them. It was the last day of school, and they were happy.

They spent the next few minutes gathering their backpacks and all their papers from their cubbies. The principal came over the loudspeaker, wishing them all a happy, healthy and safe summer. The bell rang again.

As was their practice, the kindergarten children remained seated until Lily went to the door. Once she was there, they lined up in front of her. Each child gave her a hug and left the room. Lily and Lola followed them out to the front of the building where some climbed on buses and others waited for their parents to pick them up in the car line.

Robbie stood with his friend Michael Benning, their superhero backpacks hiked up on their shoulders.

Lily smiled as they compared rocks they'd found on the playground.

One by one, the children departed, until there were only a handful remaining.

"Are you celebrating tonight at the Ugly Stick Saloon?" Lola asked.

Lily shrugged. "I might. I haven't been since the New Year's Party. And before that, I think I went for the last Annual Bachelor Auction."

Lola sighed loudly. "They don't have those nearly often enough."

Lily crossed her arms over her chest and tapped her toe. "Lola, isn't Daniel enough of a man you don't need to buy another at the auction?"

"Of course," she said. "But it doesn't hurt to look." She grinned. "A good-looking, shirtless man is like a piece of…"

"Lola…"

"Art. A piece of art." She shot a frown at Lily. "Get your mind out of the gutter, little girl."

Two trucks pulled up in the drive.

A man Lily recognized as Trevor Benning,

Michael's father, got out of the first one and walked toward Michael.

"Uh oh, we've got a problem." Lily moved to stand between Michael and his father.

"Why? What's going on?" Lola asked, her gaze darting from Lily to Trevor.

Trevor stopped in front of Lily, his eyes narrowing. "Mikey, get in the truck."

"Mama said I wasn't supposed to go with you," Michael said.

"I'm telling you to get in the truck," Trevor said, his tone deep and angry.

Lily lifted her chin. "Mr. Benning, I'm sorry, but I'm not allowed to let you take Michael from the school. We were given a copy of the restraining order. You're not even supposed to come within twenty yards of Michael." Though her heart hammered hard in her chest, Lily presented her calmest demeanor. "I'm going to have to ask you to leave the school property."

"That's my kid. Get out of my way, or I'll have to move you out of my way." He took a threatening step forward.

Robbie jumped in front of Lily. "You be nice to Miss Grayson," he demanded, his chin held high and his shoulders squared.

Lily rested her hands on Robbie's shoulders and eased him back behind her with Michael. "Thanks, Robbie, but I can handle this."

Trevor's lips curved into a thin, mean smile. "You gonna move, or am I gonna have to go through you?"

Lily didn't budge. "Lola, take the boys back a few steps. I don't want them to get hurt."

"Only one gonna get hurt around here is you, if you don't move out of my way." Benning stepped another foot closer and stared down his nose at Lily.

"Trust me, you don't want to do this," Lily said in a low, warning tone. "Go home, Trevor." She didn't back down an inch. If he wanted a fight, she was ready.

When Trevor reached out to shove her aside, she grabbed his arm and slammed him to the ground, twisting his arm up between his shoulder blades.

Lily leaned close to his ear. "I told you that you didn't want to do that."

"Get off of me, bitch." Trevor twisted and writhed beneath her.

Lily pushed his arm up higher between his shoulder blades. "Lola, call the sheriff."

Lola was already on the phone with 911 dispatch. She ended the call. "They're on their way."

A tall, dark-haired, absolutely gorgeous man raced up to her and asked, "Do you need help?"

Lily had Trevor where she wanted him. "If I needed help, I'd ask for it." She grunted as Trevor bucked beneath her. "What I need is for the sheriff to come collect this man." She looked at Robbie and Michael's scared faces. "And see? Even you guys can protect yourselves, if you know how." She gave them a strained smile. "Sorry, Michael. I couldn't let him take you."

Michael's eyebrows drew together. "I know. My daddy isn't supposed to be here," he said. "He hits my mama." He didn't cry or appear mad at her for tackling his father and forcing him to lay face-down on the ground. In fact, he appeared relieved that he didn't have to go with the man.

Sirens sounded in the distance, getting louder as they approached the school. Soon, a sheriff's vehicle pulled up, and her brother, Nash, climbed out of the SUV and stood for a moment, staring down at his sister. "Whatcha got there, Lily?"

"I can tell you what your little sister has. A whole can of whoop-ass!" Lola shook her head with a grin. "We need to pick up where we left off on my training. You've gotta teach me that Krav Maga trick."

Nash squatted down beside the man beneath Lily. "Now, Trevor, we've been over this before. We have a restraining order that says you can't be anywhere near your ex-wife or your kid. Did you forget that?" Nash cocked an eyebrow.

"Shut the fuck up, Grayson. And get the bitch off me. I want her charged with assault," Benning threatened.

Nash pulled out handcuffs. "I'm sure an attorney would love to take your money." He snapped the cuffs onto Trevor's wrists. "You can get up now, Lily. I'll take it from here."

Lily rose from the ground and dusted off her hands and the knees of her trousers. "Thanks, Officer Grayson."

Then she turned to Michael and Robbie.

The tall, dark-haired man who'd asked her if she needed help stood with the boys, one hand on Robbie's shoulder.

Lily frowned. "Are you here to pick up one of the children?"

The man held up his hands as if in surrender. "I promise I don't have a restraining order out on me. But I'm here to collect Roberto. My son." His spoke perfectly good English with a slight Hispanic accent. He held out his hand. "Do you make it a habit of attacking fathers here to pick up their children?"

Lily took his hand hesitantly. When she gripped it, a flash of heat ripped up her arm and through her body. Shocked, she yanked away her hand and rubbed it along her pant leg. "Benning isn't supposed to be around Michael. Last time he was with his family, he hurt his ex-wife and son," Lily explained. Then she dropped to one knee in front of Michael. "Are you okay?"

He sniffled, and a giant tear rolled out of the corner of one eye. "I want my mommy."

Lily glanced up as a silver car rolled into the parking lot. "She's here."

The driver's door opened, and Michael's mother jumped out. "Oh, my God! Michael!" She ran to the little boy and snatched him up in her arms. "Are you okay? Did he hurt you?"

Michael shook his head.

"He's my son," Trevor snarled as Nash walked him to the sheriff's SUV. "I have a right to see my kid."

Michael's mother turned and glared at her ex-husband. "You lost that right when you hit him, and there's a court order that proves it."

"You're going to regret this, Ava." Trevor warned.

"Mommy," Michael said, "you should have seen Miss Grayson. She wouldn't let Daddy take me. She pushed him down on the ground."

Ava glanced at Lily, a frown twisting her brow. "You took Trevor down?" She shook her head. "How? He's so much bigger and stronger than I am. I could never fight him off. And you're smaller than me."

Lily shrugged. "I've had some training."

Ava's eyes narrowed, and she shot a glance toward Trevor. "I want you to train me. I don't ever want to feel helpless again."

"I could do that," Lily said. "I'm not sure what my summer will be like. I've got some feelers out for summer work. I'll let you know."

"Thank you." Ava hugged Michael to her. "And thank you for what you did." She tipped her head toward the sheriff's vehicle.

Ava left with Michael, and Nash left with Trevor.

Which left only Robbie, his father and Lola.

"Holy smokes, Lily." Lola leaned close to her ear. "Where'd you find him?"

Lily frowned at Lola. "I didn't find him. And he's standing right here. He can hear every word you say."

The man chuckled. "Allow me to start over. I'm Antonio Delossantos, Roberto's father. My friends call me Tony."

Lily bit down hard on her tongue to keep from telling the man how she really felt about meeting him. Instead, she couched her anger in a sweet smile. "So nice to meet you, Mr. Delossantos, especially on the *last* day of school. I'm always surprised at the level of commitment parents have toward their children's education."

"Ouch," Lola murmured. "Look out, Lily's got a bone to pick."

Lily ignored Lola's comment and raised her brows at Mr. Delossantos, daring him to explain his lack of concern over his son's education, much less feelings.

CHAPTER 2

"SEE, PAPI?" Robbie said before Tony could respond to Miss Grayson's accusing tone. "I told you Miss Grayson was awesome. Did you see the way she tackled Michael's daddy? Did you?"

"Yes, son, I did." He frowned, entirely too aware of Robbie's auburn-haired, green-eyed teacher who'd just thrown a man onto the ground and rendered him helpless. "We should be going. I have to pack for my trip."

"Where is Senora Rosa? Why isn't she here?"

"She isn't feeling well," Tony said with a sigh.

"If she's sick, how can she care for us?"

"We'll figure it out." He took his son's hand. "Come on. Your sister's in the truck."

"If Senora Rosa can't take care of us, Miss Grayson can. She doesn't have a job during the summer." Robbie turned to his kindergarten teacher.

"Can you, Miss Grayson? Can you watch me and Mari while Senora Rosa is sick?"

"I think it's a perfect opportunity for your father to spend time with you." She smiled. "In fact, he could take you to the Memorial Day celebration at the fairgrounds on Monday. There will be games, prizes and fireworks. And the carnival is set up. You could ride the Ferris wheel."

"Can we, Papi? Will you take us to the fairgrounds?"

Tony frowned. He had a lot to do on the ranch before he flew back to Costa Rica to check on his other holdings. "We'll see."

Robbie's smile fell. "That means no."

"What means no?" Tony asked.

"Every time you say, *we'll see,* it means no." His son's shoulders slumped. He looked up at Miss Grayson. "Will you be there?"

She nodded. "Yes, I will."

"I hope you have fun watching the fireworks." Robbie looked up at his father. "I'm ready to go."

The abject misery in his son's face made him rethink his schedule. He'd planned on leaving Sunday, but he could put it off until Tuesday. "Fine," he said, making a decision. "We'll go to the celebration on Monday." He ruffled his son's hair. "You'll have to help me keep up with your sister."

"Really? We get to go?" Robbie hugged him around the knees. "I'll help with Mari. I promise." He turned to Miss Grayson. "We get to go. Did you hear? We'll be there and get to see you again."

"Go get in the truck," Tony said. "I'll be right there."

"Yes, Papi." Robbie ran toward the truck parked against the curb. "Mari! Mari, we get to go to the fairgrounds." He had to climb up on the running board to reach the door handle, but he managed and pulled open the door.

Tony faced Miss Grayson, maintaining a smile but letting his eyes narrow a fraction. "Thanks. That will delay my trip by a couple days."

The teacher lifted her chin. "But think of the quality time you'll spend with your children. I'm sure they would appreciate any time they could spend with their father."

He frowned. "I get the feeling you're judging me."

She shook her head, her face a picture of innocence. "He's your son. You have to raise him how you see fit. Just so you realize... He loves you and his sister. Look through his backpack."

She turned away and hooked her arm through the arm of the other woman standing beside her in ridiculously high heels.

"Lily, aren't you going to introduce me to Robbie's father?" the other woman said.

"He's not worth it," Lily replied, loud enough Tony heard.

Anger bubbled up inside. He wanted to go after

the teacher and tell her she didn't know anything about him. Therefore, she had no basis on which to judge him. He had a ranch that didn't run itself, and businesses in the home of his parents' birth, Costa Rica. He couldn't always be there for Robbie and Mari.

Which left them with his housekeeper, Rosa, for the majority of the time, although Rosa was more than a housekeeper. She had been with Tony since Tony was a little boy. She'd been there for Marisol when she'd given birth. Rosa had been there to help Tony pick up the pieces after Marisol's death.

That didn't excuse him as a parent. Without their mother, Roberto and Mari needed their other parent to give them the love, affection and nurturing they so desperately needed.

Okay, so little Miss Perfect Grayson had struck a nerve.

He'd spend more time with his children—after he returned from Costa Rica.

He climbed into his truck and glanced into the rearview mirror at Mari, his four-year-old daughter, who looked so much like him with her dark hair and big brown eyes. And Robbie who reminded him every day of his mother, who'd been killed by the drug cartel leader, El Patron. Had she still been alive, she would have been the one raising their children while Tony worked. And he'd still be missing out on getting to know them and spending time with them.

As much as he didn't want to admit it, Miss Grayson was right.

Not only was she right, she could take care of herself, unlike Marisol. Tony was sure that if El Patron had tried to hurt Miss Grayson, she'd have given him a helluva a fight.

He was glad to know Robbie had had the benefit of a teacher like Miss Grayson, who could protect him.

With the two children excited by the prospect of going to the Memorial Day celebration at the fairgrounds on Monday, they talked all the way out to the Double Diamond Ranch. Once there, they entered the house and ran to the kitchen where Rosa usually had a nutritious dinner prepared for them.

With Rosa laid up in bed, the kitchen was empty.

Tony looked around, at a loss for what to feed the children for an afternoon snack, and beyond that, what they'd eat for dinner.

Rosa had always been there to take care of all of them, even before Marisol had been killed. Now that his housekeeper-nanny was sick, he had to fend for himself, as well as for the two children.

Thankfully, Rosa's niece was there to take care of Rosa. Tony was hopeless as a nurse.

Tony found a leftover roast in the refrigerator and sliced it up for sandwiches. Mari turned up her nose at that idea, forcing him to resort to peanut butter and jelly for her.

Once they'd finished their meal, he took them outside to check with the foreman about several of the animals Tony was concerned about.

Robbie ran ahead to the barn.

Tony kept a tight grip on Mari's hand. The little girl could get away faster than a cat with its tail on fire.

Inside the barn, he met with Caleb Johnson, his young foreman, a man who'd started working for him while he'd been in high school and stayed on after Tony's older foreman retired and moved to Florida to be closer to his sister.

Robbie was busy brushing Diego, Tony's horse, the bay gelding he'd raised from a colt. The boy easily walked under the horse's belly, and the animal didn't flinch.

At six years old, Robbie already knew how to ride. Caleb had taken the time to teach the boy. A flash of guilt niggled at the back of Tony's mind. He should have been the one to introduce his son to the joy and purpose of riding.

When he got back to Texas, he would take both of his children riding. They needed to see the land and ranch they would eventually inherit.

Then why not take them to Costa Rica where their grandparents had been raised?

He'd thought about it over the past year. El Patron was safely in prison. Tony hadn't had trouble with the cartels since he'd been instrumental in the capture of the Costa Rican cartel kingpin.

Still, he couldn't forget he'd left Costa Rica and brought his children to Texas after their mother had been murdered by El Patron. A lot had changed in Costa Rica. It had become a mecca for tourists and US ex-patriots and seemed to be safer.

On the surface.

The cartels used Costa Rica as a warehouse to stage drugs traveling from South America to Mexico, then on to US consumers. The Mexican Sinaloa Cartel had a firm hold on the drug trade, and they weren't letting go anytime soon. When El Patron had been incarcerated, they'd found someone else to warehouse the drugs in transit.

So far, his hotel in Manuel Antonio had been spared any problems. The tourism trade was strong on the west coast, and the cartels pretty much left the tourists alone.

If he had someone who could take care of the children while he conducted business, he might consider taking them with him to Costa Rica.

Mari tugged on his hand. "Papi, *puedo montar el caballo?*" When he didn't respond right away, she tugged again. "*Por favor,* Papi."

Tony looked down at his dark-haired daughter. She had a habit of speaking in Spanish, which would make it more difficult for her when she started kindergarten in the fall. Rosa spoke in Spanish much of the time with the children, whereas Tony only spoke English. He would have to make a concentrated effort over the summer to immerse her in English so that she was better prepared when school started in August.

"Do you want to ride Diego?" he asked in English.

She smiled and nodded. "*Si*, Papi."

"Yes," he gently reminded her.

"Yes, Papi," she mimicked.

He lifted her up and placed her on Diego's back.

"Would you like to ride, Robbie?" he asked his young son.

"Please," the boy said with a grin.

Tony swung his son up onto the back of the animal behind his sister.

Taking the lead rope, he led Diego out of the barn and around the barn yard for several laps.

The smile on his daughter and son's faces tugged at his heart. He missed them when he was away. Perhaps he really should consider taking them to Costa Rica this time. He wondered if Rosa would be up to traveling so soon after her illness. He'd check with her after he put the children to bed that night. He wouldn't mention anything to them until he was certain he had someone to care for them while he conducted business.

If Rosa wasn't well by the time he planned to leave, he couldn't leave with or without them. If he took them with him, he had to have someone to care for them when he was busy, and as a backup, in case something happened. Someone he trusted.

His thoughts went to the little teacher who'd taken down a big man as if it had been child's play. That's the kind of caregiver his children needed if they were to go to Costa Rica with him. He wondered if he could hire someone from a bodyguard firm. Preferably, one who was good with children.

He'd check around and see what he could find. He had the number of a mercenary firm where he could hire trained military men to protect the perimeter of his holdings. He'd gotten the number from an expatriot in Costa Rica who'd hired the firm to help him protect his bar from cartel members bent on putting him out of business.

Tony wondered if the mercenary group had female mercenaries. Then again, maybe mercenaries weren't what he needed to watch over his children.

After the horseback ride, Tony took Mari and Robbie to visit the mare that had foaled that week. By the time they returned to the house, the sun was setting, and the children were tired from an exciting day.

Tony saw to it they were bathed and tucked into bed, enjoying the little things like getting splashed by Mari and being enveloped in a wet hug from Robbie. He had missed a lot since Marisol died. Perhaps he'd been running from reminders of her.

Tony kissed both children goodnight and was blessed with still more hugs. His heart swelled with love and pride. They were good children. Marisol would be so proud of them.

After he left their rooms, he descended to the kitchen where he found Ariana, Rosa's niece stirring a pot of soup for her aunt. "I'll be here all night if you'd like me to watch the children," she offered.

"I hadn't planned on going anywhere but thank you." He looked inside the refrigerator, not sure what he wanted. He wasn't hungry, and the beer he kept chilling didn't appeal to him. Closing the door, he left the kitchen and walked down the hallway to his study. He could work on the books for the ranch or check his emails for a status report concerning his holdings in Costa Rica. When he walked around his desk to take a seat, he paused, the starlight spilling through the French doors drawing him away from his desk and computer.

He strode through the French doors, pushed them open and walked out on the porch that surrounded the sprawling ranch house.

The night sky was clear, the stars shining brightly like so many diamonds.

What should have calmed him made him even more edgy. He couldn't sit, couldn't turn on the television and lounge in his living room. He needed to keep moving.

Tony returned to the kitchen.

Ariana glanced up from pouring soup into a bowl. "Is there something I can do for you, Mr. Delossantos?"

"If the offer still stands, would you mind keeping an eye out for Mari and Robbie?"

She smiled. "I don't mind at all, since I'll be here all night. Don't feel like you have to hurry home."

"Thank you, Ariana. I'll gladly pay you for babysitting."

She shook her head. "I wouldn't think of it. You've done so much for *Tia Rosa,* it's the least I can do for you."

"Still, I know you're going to college next fall, and every college student needs extra cash for books, rent and food." He held up his hand when Ariana opened her mouth to protest. "Please. Let me."

Smiling again, she nodded. "As you wish. Now, if you'll excuse me, *Tia Rosa* is waiting. I'll check on *los ninos* when we've had our dinner."

Tony left the house, locking the door behind him.

Once in his truck, he drove toward Hellfire, not sure where he was going, only knowing he couldn't sit still. On his way there, he passed a building with trucks, cars and motorcycles crowded around it and music blaring loud enough he could hear it through the closed windows of his truck.

He passed the Ugly Stick Saloon every time he drove into Hellfire without giving it a second thought. Mostly because he passed it during the day, and it wasn't open. But it was nighttime, and the bar was hopping with people and music. He'd gone less than a tenth of a mile past the saloon when he slowed, pulled off the road and, finally, turned around.

Tony parked in the back of the saloon in the only empty spot he could find. Being a Friday night, the place was packed. He hadn't been inside since he'd been single and full of himself. He understood the Ugly Stick had since changed hands and was run by a woman, a retired stripper.

Not wanting to spend the evening alone, Tony entered the saloon, passing a large female bouncer who looked him over and checked his ID before she allowed him to proceed.

He found a stool at the bar and ordered whiskey on the rocks. After the first sip burned a path down his throat, he turned toward the room full of people. As if his eyes were drawn to her, he found the woman who'd occupied much of his thoughts since he'd picked up Robbie at school.

Miss Lily Grayson sat with the woman who'd been with her that afternoon and several men he recognized as either firemen or fellow ranchers. He knew the Grayson brothers but hadn't realized they had a younger sister until he'd met her that afternoon at Robbie's school.

It struck him that he knew so little about her, and she'd taught Robbie all year.

He had some catching up to do. Without making a conscious decision, he'd started down the path to making changes that afternoon with Robbie and Mari. Perhaps he could learn more from Robbie's teacher.

The music switched to a slower country western song. The music softened, and he could actually hear himself think. Tony set his glass on the bar, stood and started across the floor.

He hadn't gone three steps before another man leaned over Lily's shoulder and held out his hand.

She smiled up at him and took that hand, letting him draw her to her feet and into his arms. They two-stepped across the dance floor, smiling and laughing.

Tony turned back to his barstool only to discover a cowboy had taken up residence on it.

"You look like a man who missed his chance. You wanna dance?" a woman with strawberry-blonde hair and red cowboy boots stepped in front of him.

He shrugged. "Not particularly."

She frowned. "I take pride in my saloon. I don't like it when I see a customer looking so down in the mouth. Come on. Show me you know how to two-step." She waved at a tall, dark-haired man in the corner.

"Are you sure?" he asked, eyeing the frowning man. "That man doesn't look too happy about you dancing with me." Tony hadn't come to the Ugly Stick Saloon to get into a barroom fight.

"Don't worry about Jackson. He knows I love him. And he knows I love to dance, and I'll always go home with the man who brought me." She winked. "Come on. These boots haven't danced in a while. They're forgetting how. By the way, I'm Audrey Anderson Graywolf. I own the joint." She took his hand and dragged him toward the dance floor.

Lily and her partner sailed past them in a full twirl. Her eyes were bright, and her smile lit up the room.

Audrey placed one of his hands on her waist, the other in her palm. "Do you know how to two-step?"

"I'm rusty." He hadn't danced since he and Marisol got pregnant with their first child over six years ago. Having a strange woman in his arms was...unsettling.

Yet, he'd wanted to dance with Lily. What was the difference? Neither woman was Marisol, the woman he'd promised to love, honor and cherish until death.

Well, death had parted them, and Tony had forgotten how to get on with his life.

"You're Tony Delossantos, aren't you?" Audrey asked.

He nodded. "I'm sorry, should I know you?"

She shook her head. "Not if you haven't been in the Ugly Stick since I bought it. I just guessed. Some of my waitresses also work at the diner in Hellfire.

They get all dreamy-eyed when they describe you." Audrey grinned. "I can see why."

Heat filled Tony's cheeks.

"Oh, don't get your shorts in a bunch. I'm not making a play for you. I have my man, and no other will do for me."

"Then why dance with me?" he asked, his gaze going over Audrey's shoulder to Lily.

"Because you looked like a guy who needed a little help. I'm all about helping my fellow man…and woman, for that matter." She twirled herself out, tapped the man's shoulder who was dancing with Lily, took Lily's hand and twirled her toward Tony. By the time she was finished with her little dance move, Lily was in Tony's arms, and Audrey danced off with Lily's former partner.

CHAPTER 3

Lily felt that same electrical surge flow through her when her hand touched Antonio Delossantos's hand as she had the first time they'd met. Now he had her hand in his and another around her waist, sending even more confusing signals along her neuropaths. She wasn't used to it and didn't know how to react.

She stopped in the middle of the dance floor. "You don't have to dance with me, you know. Audrey is a hopeless matchmaker."

"If that's the case, why did she feel you had to dance with me? You looked perfectly content dancing with that other man."

Lily smiled. "Daniel is Lola's guy. He just knows how much I like to two-step."

Tony cocked an eyebrow. "If you like two-stepping so much, why did you stop?

Heat filled Lily's cheeks. "It wasn't your idea to

dance with me. I wouldn't want you to feel obligated."

When she tried to pull her hand free of his, he held tighter. "Actually, I was on my way across to ask you to dance, but Lola's beau got to you first."

Lily's eyes narrowed. "Really? You're not just saying that to make nice with me?"

With his finger, Tony drew and X across his chest. "What is it Robbie says…? Cross my heart?"

With a smile, Lily quit trying to pull away from Tony. "Okay, then. Show me whatcha got."

Tony had just started to lead her across the dance floor when the song ended, and the band announced they were taking a break. Someone put money in the jukebox and a lively song came over the speakers. People left their seats and crowded onto the floor, forming lines and dancing in unison.

"I'm not much good at line dancing. May I buy you a drink?" Tony asked.

Lily would be better off cutting her losses and going back to the table where her brothers and Lola were sitting. Instead, she found herself shrugging. "Sure."

He led her through the maze of tables and chairs, back to the bar where two stools had been vacated. She sat in one, and he took the other.

"What can I get you?" he asked.

Feeling the need to keep her head clear and her thoughts sharp, she answered, "Ginger ale."

His eyebrows rose, but he didn't question her choice. He ordered her drink and made it two. When their clear, sparkling drinks arrived, he lifted his to touch against her glass. "Here's to refreshing drinks and starting over."

She smiled. "I'm afraid I wasn't very friendly this afternoon."

"In a good way," he pointed out. "Michael seemed to be happy he didn't have to go with his father."

"I was talking about my comments aimed at you. It isn't my place to tell you how to raise your children." She stared down into her glass. "It's just that Robbie is a special little boy, and he wears his heart on his sleeve."

Tony nodded. "He's like his mother was, in that respect."

"Don't get me wrong, he's a tough little guy, but he loves hard and only wants to be loved in return."

"That's very insightful of you." Tony took another sip and set his glass on the bar. "Do you take as great an interest in all of your students as you do with Robbie?"

Her cheeks heated again. "I like to think so, but that wouldn't be true. I love them all, but Robbie is... well...like I said...special." She touched his arm. "In a very good way. He's smart, he learns quickly, and he cares deeply about others. You're very lucky to have him as a son."

Tony smiled. "He was very close to his mother."

"Do you mind my asking what happened to her?"

The smile straightened into a thin line He didn't answer for a long moment. When he did, his voice was harsh. "She died two years ago," he said through tight lips.

"I'm sorry," Lily said, once again reaching out to touch his arm. "It was none of my business." She slid off the barstool and gave him a sad smile. "Thank you for the drink. I hope you enjoy your summer and get to spend time with Robbie. He really is a good kid, and he loves you a lot."

"Thank you for the dance. Will I see you at the fairgrounds Monday?"

She shrugged. "Maybe." Lily weaved her way back through the crowd to the table where her brothers and Lola sat laughing and talking. Though she sat in the middle of them, she couldn't focus or tune into the conversation going on around her. She tried but couldn't keep her gaze from drifting back to the man at the bar, sitting by himself, staring into his glass of ginger ale.

He must have loved his wife dearly to still mourn her loss after two years.

Lily wondered what it felt like to love that deeply. For all her twenty-six years, she could say honestly that she'd never felt that way about any of the men she'd dated. She'd vowed that, until she did, she wouldn't marry.

While all her friends from high school and college

were getting married or had been married and were having children, she was still alone, with no boyfriend and no prospects.

She'd focused instead on traveling as much as she could, determined to visit as many places as possible. Many of her friends who were married and had children didn't go anywhere.

Lily had convinced herself she was lucky to be single and able to go whenever and wherever she wanted.

Staring across the saloon at the man sitting at the bar, mourning the love he'd lost, Lily suddenly didn't feel lucky at all.

Her brother Nash leaned toward her, a frown pulling his brows together. "What's wrong, Lily Pad?"

Lily forced a smile to her face. "Nothing. Why do you ask?"

"Don't play games with me. You know I can always tell when you're lying."

She snorted. "I'm not a little girl anymore. What? Are you going to tell Mom and Dad?"

"No," he said and laid a hand over hers on the table. "I worry about you. You're not having fun, and you seem a little down in the mouth."

She shrugged. "I'm disappointed my summer gig got cancelled. I was all set to go to Greece, and now… nothing. I'm stuck in Hellfire for the summer."

Nash squeezed her hand. "Is that so bad? You have me, Beckett, Rider and Chance. And Mom and Dad are back from their latest cruise. What more could you want?"

She gave her brother a twisted grin. "To see new and exciting places? To have an adventure?"

Lola leaned across Lily, reaching for her beer on the table. "What she needs is to fall in love and have half a dozen children of her own, instead of taking care of everyone else's children."

Lily frowned at her friend and mentor. "I don't need to have children of my own. I have twenty new children every year and the pleasure of being with children during the summer when I work as an au pair."

"Which you won't be doing this summer since that boat sank," Lola reminded her. "The offer still stands… you can work with me this summer, and I'll see what I can do to find you a man."

Nash groaned. "Lola, I think Lily would like to find her own fella."

"Well, she hasn't yet. Seems to me the girl needs a little help in that department." Lola hooked her arm through Daniel's and smiled up at him. "There's something about finding the love of your life that makes you want all of your good friends to be just as happy."

"Who said I wasn't happy?" Lily pushed to her feet. "I'm happy, dammit. And I haven't given up on finding another au pair position. The summer has barely started. The world awaits." She gave the table full of all the people she loved a flippant wave. "With that, I'll bid you adieu." Lily hurried for the door, strangely on the verge of tears and not wanting anyone to witness this strange occurrence. The only girl child and the youngest of the Graysons, Lily had grown up trying to be like her brothers, all tough and invincible. She'd always refused to shed a tear in front of them, even when she was badly hurt or had her young heart broken.

Why now? Why were tears filling her eyes and threatening to spill down her cheeks before she made it outside and into the privacy of her SUV.

At the door, Greta Sue, the bouncer, stopped her. "Hey, Lily, are you okay?"

That the big bouncer could read her face and know she was in distress was Lily's undoing. "I'm fine," she blurted and dove for the door. She barely made it through before the tears spilled down her cheeks.

What was wrong with her? She shouldn't cry over the fact her trip to Greece had been called off. She had savings. If she wanted to go badly enough, she could.

No, more than that, she didn't want to go. Not if it meant going by herself.

There it was. She was tired of being alone. What fun was it to go explore new places if she didn't have anyone to share it with? At least as an au pair, she could share the joy of exploration with the children she cared for. And she loved children, even if they weren't her own. They all needed love, and she had lots of room in her heart for all of them.

And she had room in her heart for that everlasting love she'd been waiting her entire life to find. Why had it been so elusive?

An image of the tall, dark father of her favorite pupil flashed in her mind. Her body warmed, and her fingers and waist tingled where his hands had been earlier. What would it feel like to be loved by a man like that? A man who'd loved his wife so much, he still mourned her two years postmortem.

TONY CLOSED his eyes and pinched the bridge of his nose, feeling a headache coming on and wondering why he'd bothered to stop at the saloon he and Marisol had come to so long ago. The saloon was different. Not in a bad way. Some of the people were the same, and some were different. But mostly, he had changed. He wasn't the young, carefree man he'd been when he'd been dating Marisol. He barely knew that man. In fact, he could have been someone else entirely.

Leaving the saloon, he drove to Hellfire and marveled at how the town seemed to roll up the sidewalks at six o'clock in the evening and keep them rolled up until eight o'clock the next morning. The only signs of life were the lights in the windows of the houses. Everyone who wasn't at the Ugly Stick Saloon was tucked into their homes with their families, getting ready for bed if not already in them, some making love. Others simply snuggling.

Tony sighed, turned around and drove back out to the Double Diamond Ranch where his family was. As much as he loved his children, and they were everything to him, his life had never felt quite as incomplete as it did tonight.

He entered his house, let Ariana know he was home and climbed the stairs.

He entered Mari's room and tucked her in with her favorite blanket, marveling at how much she'd grown since her mother's untimely death. Marisol would've been delighted at how beautiful her little girl had become.

Then he went into Robbie's room and found him with his cheek resting on his hands, curled up in the middle of his bed. On the nightstand lay a stack of his school papers he must have brought home in his backpack. By the limited glow of the nightlight, Tony flipped through all the pictures he'd drawn. In most, he'd drawn a little boy, a smaller girl and a tall, dark-haired man, standing at a distance from the children.

Had he been that distant with his children?

Tony thought back over the past two years, and his chest squeezed so tightly it caused him physical pain.

He'd been so busy keeping busy to escape the pain

of losing Marisol, he'd left behind the two people he cared most about.

He flipped to the last of the drawings and found the same dark-haired man, little boy, little girl and a woman with orange hair and green eyes. He shot a glance toward his son, wanting to wake him and ask what the picture meant? Did Robbie want his teacher to be a more permanent part of his life?

Tony straightened the pictures and laid them on the nightstand where he'd found them. They'd been more revealing than he'd thought a six-year-old could portray. He vowed never to underestimate his son again, and to make up for the two years he'd been in a blue funk over the death of his wife. Every time he'd considered dating, he'd been struck by a guilt so strong he'd walked away from the idea.

Marisol had died. He hadn't. And his children obviously needed him.

Tony left Robbie's room and entered his own. The king-sized bed looked so big and empty. Could he ever share it with another woman? The bed he'd shared with his wife? The duvet and curtains were the ones Marisol had chosen. The soft antique blue had been soothing when they'd first had them made and installed. Now, they seemed more depressing than soothing. Marisol had even chosen the modern white furniture. The furniture suited her. Not him. He liked to see the grain of wood. Stained furniture felt warm and had more character than the sleek, shiny white finish of the nightstands and dresser.

Perhaps he needed to make changes. Drastic changes. Before he left for Costa Rica, he'd hire an interior designer and have her start the transformation. To get on with his life, he had to let go of the past.

With a new direction in mind, he showered and dropped into his bed, willing sleep to come quickly. And it did, but not before a certain auburn-haired teacher flashed into his thoughts, determined to invade his dreams.

By morning, he was so hard he had to shower again to calm his urges and get his head on straight. He spent a good part of Saturday with an interior designer he found through a friend of Ariana's. She came to the house and walked through every room, asking him what his preferences were and what colors made him happy. He involved Robbie and Mari when it came to their rooms and the living room they shared. By the time the woman left, Tony was ready to climb the walls. Instead, he saddled up his horse and a pony for Robbie. With Mari riding in front of him in his saddle and Robbie on his pony beside him, they went on a trail ride through the ranch, stopping to have a picnic by a stream.

They enjoyed the afternoon wading in the water and chasing tadpoles. By the time they headed back to the house, Mari was so sleepy she fell asleep against Tony. Back at the barn, Robbie insisted on brushing his own mount, while Caleb took care of Tony's.

Tony carried Mari upstairs and helped her with her bath and into her pajamas.

Once Robbie had his shower, they sat down to a meal Ariana had prepared of tacos, refried beans and rice.

Then Tony curled up on the sofa with Robbie and Mari and watched a Disney cartoon movie until all three of them fell asleep, exhausted from the day of adventure.

Later that night, Tony carried Mari up to her room and came back down to carry Robbie.

Robbie woke long enough to wrap his arms around his father's neck. "Thank you for today. Miss Grayson says we should remember the days we love most, so that when it's raining or we're sad, we have a memory to cheer us up."

Tony's heart swelled as he laid his son in his bed and pulled the blankets up around him. "Are you planning on rain or being sad?"

Robbie nodded. "When you leave to go to Costa Rica, I'll have today to remember when I'm sad." He hugged his father's neck. "Thank you, Papi."

Tony pressed a kiss to his son's forehead, his gut clenching at his son's words. "I love you, Roberto."

He yawned and closed his eyes, murmuring, "Mama used to call me Roberto."

"It's your name," he reminded him.

Tony's son turned on his side and tucked his hands beneath his cheek, his eyes firmly closed. "I like it when Miss Grayson calls me Robbie." And on that last word, his voice faded, and he fell asleep.

There she was again. Lily Grayson, popping up in his son's thoughts as well as his. He turned off the light on the nightstand and left Robbie's room to return to his own.

He'd gone the entire day, filling it with memories with Robbie and Mari. All the while, he'd worked hard not to allow a certain auburn-haired, kickass female from intruding on his day. And, for the most part, he'd been successful.

Until Robbie brought her front and center to his thoughts. Right before he went to bed. How the hell was he supposed to sleep when his body was on fire with a need and desire he hadn't known he'd missed for the past two years.

All because of a sassy teacher who could take him down if he so much as pissed her off.

He vowed to spend all of Sunday Lily-free, working his ranch and making sure he didn't leave Caleb with any headaches he couldn't handle on his own.

He'd decide what to do with the children on Monday. Hopefully, Rosa would be well enough to resume their care. If not, maybe Ariana?

Whatever happened, he had to make the trip to

Costa Rica. He'd been away for three months. Any time he was gone longer than three months without checking in, things seemed to fall apart. Though the hotel manager was quite capable, the staff needed his direction and insight. He'd taken what his parents had started and had grown it into a high-class resort, worthy of celebrity visits. But it required hands-on guidance by phone, video conferencing and—most importantly—being there.

Which meant leaving his children, yet again.

Lily's words hit him again. His children had lost their mother. Having one parent around was better than none.

Tony lay in his bed long into the night. thinking through his options. In the wee hours of the morning, he finally fell asleep and immediately dreamed of a spunky redhead throwing him to the ground and making mad, passionate love to him.

When he woke, he was disappointed to find the pillow beside him empty.

CHAPTER 4

LILY SPENT the weekend hitting up all her contacts, searching for another position as an au pair for the summer. Every lead landed in a dead end. Most people reserved their au pair ahead of the summer. They were already flying off to exotic locations with someone else, not Lily.

By Monday morning, she was facing the fact she'd be stuck in Hellfire for the summer. She loved her family, but she saw them throughout the school year. And Lily loved visiting new and exciting countries. There might be a day when she married and had children of her own, at which time, she wouldn't get to travel as much, and probably wouldn't want to. Now, in the prime of her life, while she was ready, willing and physically capable, she wanted to travel…just not alone.

It wasn't the fear of being accosted; it was more a

fear of being alone. She'd grown up in a houseful of people. Her four older brothers had made certain their lives weren't boring. If she'd ever needed a shoulder to lean on, her father, mother or one of the boys had been there.

Perhaps she could talk Lola into going on a trip with her. Maybe they could hop on a cruise ship for a couple of weeks or fly down to the Virgin Islands and snorkel and laze on a beach.

The more she thought about it, the more she liked that idea. So, it wouldn't be for the entire summer as she'd planned, but it would be better than staying in Hellfire as the sun heated the dry Texas town.

She was due to meet up with Lola and Daniel at the Memorial Day celebration at the fairgrounds that afternoon. If Tony Delossantos could be believed, he might be there with his son and daughter. Her heart fluttered. The man was infuriating, but still the most interesting thing about the day she had planned. Not that she was going to flirt with him. The man clearly wasn't over the death of his wife. Lily didn't want to be a rebound notch on the wealthy man's bedpost. She'd spend her time convincing Lola that she needed a vacation away from the shoe store. She could shut it down for two weeks or have one of her staff run it while she was gone. Being a business owner, Lola could take off when she wanted. After all, she was the boss.

Her firefighter beau, however, wasn't quite as

flexible. He would have to put in for time off. And really, Lily would want Lola to herself. Someone to share a cabin with. If Daniel came, he and Lola would want to be alone in a cabin of their own. Which would defeat the purpose of Lily taking Lola on the voyage.

Lily was glad for her friends and family, but she wanted time away from Hellfire, exploring, seeing the world.

The celebration at the fairgrounds started at noon and would last until after sunset that night when the fireworks would begin.

Her brothers would all be there with their women, and Lola would have Daniel. They always included her on public outings but, just once, it would be nice to have a date of her own.

Lily rode with her brother Beckett and his fiancée, Kinsey. They brought along a big basket of food to share with the rest of the family and a couple of blankets to lay out on when the fireworks started.

The fairgrounds were hopping with booths and activities for the children, games for the adults, and the carnival had been set up in the big field where a Ferris wheel and tilt-o-whirls spun children until they barfed.

The sun was out with a few of the big cotton-candy clouds that made the sky so pretty in the summer.

Though she didn't have the job she'd wanted for

the summer, Lily couldn't help but smile and join in the fun. She challenged Beckett to swing the mallet and ding the bell. Twice, he rang the bell, and she didn't. On her third try, she made the metal pin slam to the top and rang the bell. Elated at her little victory, she turned to see Robbie chasing after his little sister, his father nowhere in sight.

Lily handed the mallet to her brother Nash. "Your turn. I have to check on something." And she ran after Robbie.

The little guy had just caught up to his sister, who was giggling and laughing, trying to squirm out of her brother's grip.

"Mari," Robbie said through gritted teeth, struggling to maintain his hold. "You have to stay with me, or you'll get lost."

"*Quiero jugar*," she said and wiggled free. She took off in the opposite direction from her brother and ran into Lily.

Lily reached down and plucked her up into her arms. "Well, what have we got here?" She smiled down at the prettiest little girl she'd ever seen. She had glossy black curls that almost had a blue tinge and the biggest brown eyes fringed in thick black lashes.

"*Mi nombre es Mari*," she said. "*Tengo cuatro años*." She held up four little fingers.

Though the little girl spoke in Spanish, Lily

understood. Her name was Mari, and she was four years old.

"Hi, Mari." Lily dipped her head toward Robbie as he came to a skidding halt in front of her. "Is this your brother?"

Mari nodded. *"Eso es Robbie. Él es mi hermano."*

"And are you supposed to stay with your brother?" Lily asked.

Mari's eyes widened, and she nodded.

"Papi is gonna be mad," Robbie said, a scowl marring his smooth forehead. "He'll never bring us back to the carnival again."

"I'm sure he'd understand," Lily reassured them. "Let's go find him before he calls out the search dogs to find his children."

Robbie's eyes rounded. "He'd call out the search dogs?" The little boy shook his head. "We're going to be in big trouble."

Mari's eyes welled with tears. *"Problema."*

"Hey, hey. There will be no crying when Miss Grayson is holding you. You wouldn't want to get my pretty new blouse wet, would you?" Lily touched the emerald green fabric. "Do you like this color?"

Mari nodded.

"What color is it?"

The little girl shook her head and buried her face against Lily's shoulder.

Lily turned to Robbie. "Does your sister speak any English?"

"Only when she wants to," he replied. "She gets to go to kindergarten when school starts back. Maybe she'll be in your class."

Lily's brow twisted. The child didn't speak English? Robbie had never spoken Spanish in her class. How was it that his sister wasn't as fluent in English as her brother?

Lily had another bone to pick with Robbie's dad. She glanced around, searching a sea of faces for the one so much like his daughter's.

When she spotted him, her knees grew weak, and she broke out in a sweat. He hadn't even turned in her direction yet. When he did, her heart fluttered, and she thought she might have to run.

How did the man have such an impact on her?

If she could, she'd set Mari on her feet, point her in her father's direction, and then Lily would turn and run as far and as fast as she could.

In the end, Lily walked slowly toward him and waited for the man to face her with his inky black-brown eyes. As she drew closer, she feared her knees might fail her altogether.

TONY'S HEART beat so hard in his chest he couldn't catch his breath. It had been at least three minutes since he'd last seen Robbie or Mari. How had this happened? They were two children with short legs.

How could they get away from him so fast and be gone for so long?

He'd been standing at one of the food trucks, ordering a funnel cake and lemonade for Robbie. He'd given his son strict instructions to hold onto Mari's hand and not let go. For exactly thirty seconds he'd glanced away. When he'd turned back, both of his children had disappeared into the crowd of people who'd assembled from all over the tri-county area surrounding Hellfire.

All Tony could see was adults with their hands on their children. No Robbie and no Mari. He knew he should have kept them at home, safe on the ranch where they knew their boundaries, and he knew their hiding places.

Tony was on the verge of shouting for everyone to stop where they were and look for his children when he spied Nash Grayson, an off-duty sheriff's deputy. If anyone could help him, Nash could.

He strode up to the cowboy and the woman whose hand was hooked around his elbow. "Please," he said, trying to hold back the desperation threatening to overwhelm him. "I can't find my children."

Grayson's brow drew together in a deep V, and he got right down to business. "How old are they, what do they look like and what are they wearing?"

"Robbie is six with brown hair and green eyes. He's wearing a superhero T-shirt, jeans and cowboy boots. Mari is four years old with black hair and brown eyes. She's wearing a pink and white shirt with ruffles on the shoulders and pink shorts.

"When was the last time you saw them?" Grayson asked.

Tony ran his hand through his hair, staring around at the crowd before him. "Approximately three minutes ago."

"Where?"

"By the funnel cake booth." He jerked his thumb over his shoulder toward the stand where he'd abandoned the confectionary delight and the ice-cold lemonade he'd been salivating over. He couldn't even think about food when his children could be in danger.

Nash pulled out his cellphone. "I'll get my brothers to start looking right now. Then we can go to one of the carnies and ask to use their loudspeaker system."

"Anything, just hurry. Someone could have snatched them, or they could have wandered too close to one of the big rides."

Nash hit the buttons on his phone and pressed it to his ears. "Beckett, I've got Tony Delossantos with me. He's missing a couple of kids."

"Did I hear someone say they were missing a couple of kids?" a familiar female voice sounded behind Tony.

He spun to face Lily. In her arms was Mari, her

head lying on Lily's shoulder, a mischievous smile curving her lips.

Beside Lily stood Robbie, his hand in hers, his eyes wide and scared. "I'm sorry, Papi. Mari let go of my hand and ran. I tried to catch her and bring her back, but she thought we were playing." He shrank a little behind Lily. "You aren't mad, are you?"

Tony drew in a deep, steadying breath and dropped to a squat beside his young son. "Roberto, I'm not angry. I was scared I'd lost you." He pulled his son into his arms and held him tight. "I know you tried. Mari can be a little handful. Thank you for staying with her. You are my hero."

Robbie smiled up at his father. "Really?"

Tony nodded and straightened.

"Never mind," Nash Grayson was saying on the phone. "Lily found them. Call off the Amber alert. All is well." He ended the call and grinned at Tony. "I'm guessing these are the children you were looking for?"

Tony nodded and held out his arms for Mari. "Come on, *chiquita*."

Mari shook her head and buried it against Lily's neck. "No, Papi. *Yo quiero señorita Lily*."

"Use your English, Mari," Tony reminded his daughter gently.

"No, Papi." Mari clung to Lily, refusing to let go.

Short of prying her loose, Tony didn't know what else to do.

"If it's okay with you, I don't mind keeping an eye on her," Lily said. "She's no bother."

Tony arched an eyebrow. "I'm not sure you know what you're up against. She's a master at disappearing."

Lily smiled. "I've been teaching kindergarten for the past four years. I'm pretty good at keeping up with the best of the hiding children."

"I'll leave you two to figure out the children," Nash said. "Kinsey wants me to help her pick a picnic spot for the family." He raised a brow and turned to his sister. "See you later this afternoon? Text me if you want to know where. And Tony, you and the kids are welcome to join us. I think Kinsey packed enough food for all of Hellfire."

"I'll be there," Lily said.

"Thank you," Tony said.

Nash took off toward a field of freshly mown grass, leaving Tony alone with Lily and his two children.

"So, we meet again," Tony said. "Since my daughter seems to be permanently attached to your shoulder, can I interest you in a drink? Ginger ale, isn't it?"

She shook her head. "Only at bars. I would love a lemonade."

"Done. I was in the process of securing said lemonade for myself and the kids, when the Houdinis performed their heart-stopping disappearing act. I'm beginning to think child leashes aren't nearly as bad as their reputation." He would have taken her arm, but Mari was using one and Robbie held Lily's other hand.

Upstaged by his own children.

At least he'd found them. Or rather, Lily had. For a moment there, he'd thought someone had absconded with them. He didn't advertise his wealth, but he was a very rich man. Not only did he have a working ranch in Texas and a hotel in Costa Rica, he had many other business pursuits, not to mention the money he'd invested wisely in the stock market. Anyone could have taken them and demanded a sizeable ransom.

And Tony would have paid it to get them back.

He waved a hand toward the food truck. "After you."

Lily, holding Mari on one arm and Robbie's hand with her other, fell in step with Tony.

"Apparently, I need to work on keeping track of small children in a public place," Tony admitted.

"True."

"My housekeeper usually takes charge of them. She's quite good at it. She has been with me since I was Robbie's age."

"Where is she now?"

"She has been sick."

Lily's brow furrowed. "Is she going to be all right?"

"The doctor said she had walking pneumonia, but that she's on the mend. My problem is that I need to go to Costa Rica tomorrow, and I'm afraid to leave the children with Rosa while she's still recovering."

"Then take them with you."

Lily made it sound so easy.

"You don't understand. I don't have childcare there. I trust only Rosa with Robbie and Mari. I wouldn't leave them with strangers."

"Then you need to postpone your trip until Rosa is well." She gave him a twisted smile. "It's not rocket science."

"Can we go to Costa Rica with you, Papi?" Robbie asked. "I want to go. I haven't been since mama took us."

And that was a problem. Bringing Robbie and Mari would stir up more memories than Tony cared to recall. He was just getting past the sorrow and guilt. Seeing his children where they'd last been with their mother was bound to dredge up old memories.

"Please, Papi," Robbie begged. "Take us with you."

"I can't," Tony said. "Rosa isn't well. She can't come right now."

Robbie's forehead wrinkled. "We don't have to take Rosa; we can take Miss Grayson."

Lily gasped and held up her hand. "I can't go to Costa Rica tomorrow."

"If not tomorrow, how about the next day?" As usual, Robbie was a persistent little guy. He went after what he wanted and didn't take no for an answer.

At any other time, Tony would have admired that tenaciousness.

"Please, Miss Grayson."

Already she was shaking her head. "I can't," Lily repeated. "Besides, your father wouldn't want me along." She shot a glance toward the man.

Tony cupped his chin, pretending to think hard on what his son had suggested. He couldn't leave the children with a sick housekeeper. And he didn't know who he could trust in Costa Rica who was good with children and could defend them if someone tried to hurt or take them.

Based on what he'd seen of Lily, so far, she could do the job. She came from a good family. Everyone in Hellfire knew the Graysons. She was a teacher, and she had some fighting skills.

Finally, the most important factor was Robbie and Mari seemed to like her.

"You know, Robbie, you might be on to something." Tony turned to Lily. "Miss Grayson, do you have plans for this summer?" He didn't wait for his response, already shaking his head. "Of course, you have plans. An independent young woman such as you will always have plans." He turned away and stared at the crowd of people gathered for the day's festivities. "Never mind."

For a long moment, Lily, Mari and Robbie didn't say anything.

Then a small hand slipped into Tony's.

He looked down at his son with those green eyes so like his mother's. "Papi, you have to ask her really nice."

"No, you don't," Lily commented. "I can't go to Costa Rica,"

He caught her gaze and held it. "Why not?"

"I…I…I don't know you well enough." She shifted Mari to her other arm.

"You are a teacher, no?"

"Yes, I am."

"How many of your students do you know when the school year begins?"

"None of them."

"But you give them the benefit of the doubt and get to know them."

"True. But they are, for the most part, harmless." She lifted one shoulder. "Except Johnny Austin. He bit. You, Mr. Delossantos are a full-grown adult. I'd be going to a foreign country with little or no information about the man I would be accompanying. I'd be stupid or a fool to go without performing a thorough background check. I do that with all my clients before I go to foreign countries with them."

Tony cocked an eyebrow. "You do this often? Go with people you don't know to other countries?"

She frowned. "I've worked for the past four

summers as an au pair. I travel with a family and watch their children while they visit or vacation in other countries. I help them, they pay my way, and the children and I get to see a lot of new and interesting places. It's a win-win situation all around."

Tony spread his arms wide. "So, what's the difference? I would hire you as an au pair to my children, whom you already know. I would pay your way to Costa Rica and pay you as you work taking care of Robbie and Mari."

"I can't," Lily said, her voice faint.

Mari wrapped her arms around her neck and snuggled closer.

Lily turned her face and deposited a kiss on the child's cheek.

The gesture was so natural and beautiful, it caught Tony by surprise. For a moment, he forgot what he was arguing about. When he recalled, he wanted to secure her agreement to accompany them even more. "Mari likes you. She doesn't like everyone."

"If she's starting kindergarten next fall, someone needs to work on getting her to speak in English. It will make her transition easier."

He waved his hand. "There you go. You're just the person she needs. In Costa Rica, everyone there will be speaking Spanish. She will have little chance to practice her skills in English, unless you accompany her there and use your most excellent teaching practices with her. With your help, she'll be ready for kindergarten next fall."

Lily's frown deepened. "I can't."

He crossed his arms over his chest. "Can't or won't?" Tony pointed toward his son, whose face was sad and pleading. "You wouldn't disappoint a little boy, would you?"

Lily's eyes narrowed. "You're not playing fair," she whispered.

"I like to get my way." He lifted his chin, unapologetically. "Do you have another position as an au pair keeping you from going with us to Costa Rica?"

She bit down on her bottom lip as if she wanted to say yes but couldn't lie. Finally, she sighed. "No."

"Then, can I count on you to help me with my children by spending the summer in beautiful Costa Rica, where you will have access to sun, sand and the ocean as your playground?" he asked in front of his children, knowing it would make it even harder for her to say no.

"We're all going to Costa Rica?" Robbie asked and held his breath, waiting for the answer.

Tony tilted his head, waiting for Lily to respond.

She drew in a deep breath and let the air out before she nodded. "Yes."

CHAPTER 5

"MISS GRAYSON, we're about to land in San José," a deep male voice sounded near her ear.

The resonance in Tony's voice, and the way he enunciated her name with that hint of a Spanish accent, sent shivers across Lily's skin.

She looked away from the window she'd been staring through since they'd crossed the Gulf of Mexico and passed over the Yucatan Peninsula, Honduras and Nicaragua. The plane slowed and came down in altitude until she could see the terrain a little better. Soon, they were flying over houses as they entered the airspace over San José.

She had to admit the flight was one of the best she'd ever been on. The chartered jet held only Delossantos, his children and her. A pilot, co-pilot and a flight attendant completed the flight crew. They had all been so helpful getting them settled into the plush white leather seats, feeding them and getting them whatever they might want to drink. The children each had their own video display monitors and could watch whatever shows or movies they wished.

Mari had fallen asleep soon after they'd taken off from the little airport on the outskirts of Hellfire. They were two hours into the flight before Robbie succumbed to slumber.

As the plane circled the airport, both children woke and looked out the windows.

Mari was excited because Robbie was excited. She was too young to really understand that they'd traveled to a foreign country, but she knew about flying in planes and hadn't run all over the plane making a nuisance of herself.

Lily gathered her things, and then white-knuckle-gripped the armrests as the plane touched down on the tarmac.

The pilot was good and made the plane kiss the concrete with the wheels before coming to a full stop in front of the main aviation terminal.

They disembarked, passed through customs relatively quickly, stopped for a bathroom break and were met outside by a driver with a black SUV.

Their luggage was stowed in the back of the vehicle, and before she could make heads or tails of the streets of San José, they were out of the city and driving through the countryside, traveling west on a highway.

The driver had brought with him food for them to eat on the trip to the coast.

As she nibbled on a sandwich, Lily stared out at the hills, valleys, grasslands and forests. Soon they were headed south, paralleling the coastline. The water was so blue and inviting, Lily could hardly wait to take Robbie and Mari out to wade in the ocean.

By the time they reached the hotel in Manuel Antonio, they had been traveling more than eight hours.

The children were fussy and out of sorts, and Lily couldn't wait to get to her room to shower and change into one of the sundresses she'd brought with her.

The weather was warm and humid outside, but once they were inside the hotel, air conditioning chilled the rooms, making her more comfortable.

A beautiful woman in a smart, gray suit met them as they entered the bright, breezy lobby. She had dark brown hair, brown eyes and a curvy figure that fit perfectly in her skirt suit. "*Buenos días, Señor* Delossantos. We're so very pleased to see you."

"Good to see you, too," he said, holding out his hand to shake the woman's. "I trust you are well?"

She nodded.

Tony turned to Lily. "Bianca Reyes is the hotel manager. Bianca, this is Lily Grayson. She is here to care for Roberto and Mari. See to it that she is given anything she needs for herself and the children."

"*Si, Señor,*" Bianca said.

"I'll need copies of the balance sheet, profit and loss statements and stats on occupancy rates. After I get my family settled in their rooms, I'll expect those reports to be in my office when I come down."

"Yes, sir," the woman said, her brow pinched. "We weren't aware you'd be bringing your children with you. The spare bedroom in your suite is set up with two beds. We'll have another bed brought up for the au pair. Where would you like it to be placed?"

Tony waved a hand, his lips pressing into a thin line. "I'll let Miss Grayson decide." He stepped away from the hotel manager and greeted a man dressed in a white guayabera shirt, long, baggy shorts and flipflops.

"If there's a couch or sofa in the living area, I can sleep on it." Lily smiled. "I'm easy to please. But I would like a pillow and some blankets, please."

Bianca nodded. "As you wish. How long can we expect you and the children to be here?"

Lily's smile spread into a grin. "All summer."

By the woman's stiff expression, she didn't appear to share Lily's enthusiasm. Instead, she turned, walked to the concierge desk and gave the bellhop instructions in Spanish. Soon, their luggage was removed from the back of the SUV, piled onto a rolling cart and taken to their suite at the top of the building.

Lily took a moment to glance around the lobby at the lavish furnishings, the beautiful feature against one wall that appeared to be a curtain of water, the sound soothing to weary travelers.

When Tony came back to where he'd left Lily standing, he brought the fair-haired man in the guayabera shirt with him. "Lily Grayson, this is Marcus Shipley, retired Navy SEAL. Marcus is in charge of security, pool maintenance and is the resident boat captain for Bahía Azul resort and spa. Lily is in charge of Roberto and Mari."

Marcus took Lily's outstretched hand. Instead of shaking it, he lifted it to his lips and kissed the backs of her knuckles. "The pleasure is entirely mine. Please tell me your boss will let you have time off to enjoy the beauty and excitement of Manuel Antonio."

She found his familiarity with her hand slightly annoying. Out of the corner of her eye, she noticed Tony frowning. That he found Marcus's greeting annoying made it fine with her. She gave Marcus a wide smile. "That would be nice. I have every Friday evening off and Sundays."

"Perfect. I'll take you out on the Lost Cause."

She cocked a brow. "Lost Cause?"

"My fishing boat. I contract it out to guests at the resort for day trips to where they can catch the bigger fish."

"I would love to go fishing," Lily said, warming to the idea.

"Then it's a date?"

Lily laughed. "I don't know if it's a date if you count bringing along two small children—"

"—and their father," Tony added. "If you add all that in, then it's a date."

Marcus shot a wry grin toward Tony. "Name the day, and I'll be sure not to book paying customers on the Lost Cause."

"Why did you name your boat Lost Cause?" Lily asked.

"When I separated from the Navy, I was pretty much a lost cause. Then I found Costa Rica and Tony, here."

"And the rest is history." Tony gave Marcus a curt nod then hooked Lily's arm and led her and the children toward the elevators. "Let me show you to your room."

Lily took Mari's hand. Tony held Robbie's hand and her elbow. They walked to the elevators, side by side. If anyone had been watching, they would have thought they were a family.

Something strong and poignant tugged at Lily's heart. Was it longing? With all of her friends from high school and college marrying and having babies, Lily was feeling her biological clock ticking. Not that twenty-six was ancient, but it was four years short of thirty. Then she'd be forty, and then fifty. She didn't want to get that far without having a family of her own. She'd love to have beautiful children like Robbie and Mari. Any woman would be proud to have those two to raise. If Tony ever remarried, they would be someone else's children.

Why Lily was sad just because she was thinking along those lines, she couldn't say. She barely knew Tony. Plus, Robbie was one of twenty children in her last kindergarten class. How did that make him special?

Because he was. He'd cared about the others in his classroom. He cared about his little sister and his father. The little boy had a certain love of life, along with a deep sadness about him. Lily always had the urge to grab him up in her arms and hug away his hurt and sorrow. Having lost his mother must have been really hard on him.

The elevator door dinged and slid open. Inside, the car walls were lined with mirrors. The rails were a polished stainless steel.

Lily turned to face the door. In her peripheral vision she could see Tony looking at her.

Heat rose up her neck and into her cheeks.

"How old are you, Miss Grayson?" he asked out of the blue.

Lily frowned. "Not that it's any of your business, but I'm twenty-six. Why do you ask?"

He shrugged. "I was curious as to why a beautiful

woman such as yourself is unmarried and caring for children not her own."

Lily's frown turned upside down. "That's easy. I haven't met a man I care enough about to commit the rest of my life to. I like children, and I like to travel in the summertime. I don't make a lot of money as a teacher, but I have my summers to do as I please. As an au pair, I get to see a lot of interesting places for free, and I'm being paid."

"Have you ever been in love?"

Lily raised her eyebrows and stared at the man. "Again…not your business."

He held up his hands. "My apologies. I'm just curious."

The elevator bell rang, saving Lily from an immediate response. The doors opened, and they stepped out before she replied. "Once, I thought I was in love. He didn't love me."

"How do you know he didn't love you?"

"It was all about control. He had to be in control. And he wanted me to change to accommodate his need to control." Her lips tightened. "I believe marriage is a partnership. One person does not have the right to control the other. They go into the relationship knowing what they're getting and willing to accept each other, faults and all."

TONY FROWNED. Lily's ex-boyfriend sounded like a

dick. "He wasn't willing to let go of yours or admit to his own faults?"

Lily snorted. "No."

Tony had no time to ponder her unsettling words. They arrived in front of a set of grand double doors.

Using a card key, Tony unlocked and opened the doors. He threw them wide, and then stepped back. "Welcome to your home away from home while you are here in Costa Rica."

Lily gasped as she stepped into the penthouse suite. Everything in it was black and white, from the white sectional sofa to the black granite bar and beyond. Cathedral ceilings stretched high above them, and windows rose from the floor to the roof, displaying a stunning view of the deep blue ocean.

"Wow," Lily whispered. "This is gorgeous."

"I'm glad you like it."

"I love it." She winced and glanced around at the white furniture and flooring. "Is it practical with children?"

He nodded. "I made certain the furnishings and flooring were childproof. The fabric of the sofas and chairs are treated to be stain resistant. And the flooring is white marble, also stain resistant and strong."

Robbie ran from room to room, Mari following. He appeared in a doorway. "This room is huge, Miss Grayson. It's got a big bed, another couch, a bathroom and a giant TV." Running to the second room, he came out grinning. "This room has two big beds, a TV and its own bathroom, too." His gaze shot to his father. "Is this where me and Mari will be sleeping?"

Tony scooped Mari up into his arms. "Yes, it is," Tony said. "It will be your room until we go back to Texas."

The luggage had arrived before them and stood beside the door.

Robbie hurried to find a superhero suitcase, rolled it into the kids' room and unzipped it. One by one, he unpacked his superhero figurines and stood them on one of the two black lacquer dressers.

Mari found her princess suitcase and followed Robbie into the room. She unzipped her case and pulled out several dolls dressed in outfits with ruffles and bows. She laid them on one of the beds.

Lily laughed. "I'm glad to see they have priorities. I can store my things in their room and closet to keep them out of the way." She tipped her head toward the giant sectional sofa. "Sleeping on the couch will be no problem. It's plenty big enough to be comfortable."

Tony frowned. "You will not sleep on the couch. I will sleep on the sofa, and you can have the master bedroom to yourself."

This time, Lily raised her hands in protest. "I can't do that."

"Can't or won't," he asked.

"Look, you're here to conduct business. I'm here to have fun and play with the children. It makes sense to let you sleep comfortably." When he opened his mouth to protest, Lily held up her hand again. "Please. I wish to be closer to the children should they need me in the night. If anything, I could sleep with Mari and be perfectly fine."

Tony shook his head. "Mari sleeps like a windmill. I know. On nights with violent storms, she crawls into bed with me and kicks me all night. At the very least, I can have them deliver a comfortable cot we can set up in the living room."

She nodded. "If you insist. Although the couch looks fine to me."

"I insist." And the conversation was ended.

"Now that we've settled the sleeping arrangements, I have business to attend. You have free reign over the premises. We have a couple pools and the beach. I would like to have dinner with my children and, afterward, we can listen to music at one of our family friendly nightclubs."

Lily nodded. "I'll have the children dressed and ready for dinner. We will be eating on Texas time, right? I know a lot of Central American countries like to have late dinners."

"We'll have the evening meal on Texas time."

She nodded. "In the meantime, we probably only have time for a quick dip in the pool." She turned to Robbie and Mari's room where they were happily playing with the toys they'd brought. "What do you say, children? Wanna go swimming?"

"Yes!" Robbie yelled.

"Si!" Mari chimed in.

Lily scooped her up in her arms. "Can you say yes?"

Mari nodded. "Yes."

Lily laughed. "Very nice."

A big grin on her face, Mari repeated, "Very nice."

"Tell you what, you teach me more Spanish, and I'll help you with your English. Okay?" She held up her hand for a high five.

Mari slapped her hand against Lily's. "Okay."

Tony stood with his hand on the doorknob for a long moment. Then he left the room.

Lily's gaze followed him until the door closed behind him.

By the look in his eyes, he probably would rather have spent the afternoon with the kids by the pool.

Lily helped Robbie find his suit, helped Mari into hers, and changed into her own black one-piece in record time. She threw on a sheer, colorful coverup and a pair of sandals, and she was ready. After being cooped up in a plane and car for the majority of the day, they needed to move and burn off some energy.

The ride down the elevator took very little time. One of the front desk clerks gave her directions to the pool. Holding Mari and Robbie's hands in hers, she strolled through the building to the courtyard where a large pool was surrounded by lounge chairs. Pool toys and inflatable water wings were available at a stand in the shade. She fit a pair of water wings over Mari's and Robbie's arms, though Robbie insisted he knew how to swim.

"For the first time in this pool, I'd like you to wear them," Lily said. "Then, as you show me how well you swim, I'll think about letting you go without."

Robbie nodded. "Okay, Miss Grayson."

"And you don't have to call me Miss Grayson while we're here. You can call me Lily."

His brow wrinkled. "How about Mama Lily?"

Though her heart swelled at his request, Lily couldn't allow it. "Oh, sweetie, I'm not your mother. That wouldn't be right."

"Tia Lily?" he suggested.

She nodded. "Auntie Lily is better." She squatted down in front of Mari. "Can you call me Auntie Lily?"

Mari flung her arms around her neck. "Auntie Lily."

Lily lifted Mari in her arms and walked into the shallow end of the pool. Robbie stepped in behind her. Warmed by the tropical sun, the water was perfect. Lily waded in up to her waist with Mari until her water wings floated her little body above the surface. She hadn't asked Tony if the children had ever taken swim lessons. He was a wealthy man. For all she knew, they had a pool at home and swam like fish.

Mari laughed and splashed water in Lily's face.

Then she pushed away from Lily and swam back to the shallow end where she could put her feet on the bottom.

Lily chuckled. "So, you do know how to swim."

Robbie was all over the pool. Soon, Lily let him shed the water wings, and he dove to the bottom for plastic rings.

After an hour in the water, she dried them with big fluffy towels provided by the hotel and took them up to the room where she filled a bathtub full of bubbles and toys and let Mari play for a few minutes before she washed her hair and rinsed her. Robbie showered on his own with a little help rinsing the shampoo from his hair.

After she dressed and combed their hair, Lily settled them in their bedroom, playing with their toys. She gathered her toiletries and stepped into the shower adjoining their room. She left the door open so that she could listen for them and peek out every so often to make sure they were still there and okay.

She had just lathered her hair with the shampoo provided by the hotel when she heard a deep voice in the other room. Lily froze. The bathroom door was wide open. Only a shower curtain separated her from the all-seeing gaze of her employer. She poked her head around the edge of the curtain to see Tony standing beside Robbie, admiring his work with the Lego blocks he'd brought with him.

Quickly rinsing the soap from her hair, she

applied conditioner, rinsed and finished up. The deep voice continued to hum in the other room, the sound making Lily warm all over, even when she turned off the water and the cool breeze of the air conditioner caressed her skin.

Now what? She reached for the towel on the towel bar outside the shower but couldn't quite get her hands on it without stepping out of the shower.

Wrapping the lower edge of the shower curtain around her, she stepped out of the shower onto the smooth tile floor and leaned over to snatch the towel from the bar. When she did, the curtain rod pulled free of the wall. Because she was leaning into the curtain when the rod released, Lily lost her balance. Her feet slipped on the wet tile, and she crashed to the floor, the curtain rod smacking her in the head.

To add insult to the injury, she couldn't unwind herself from the curtain to get to her feet.

"Need a hand?" that deep familiar voice said.

"No, I do not." Pulling the towel up over her naked breasts, she tried to roll over, but the curtain rod kept the curtain from coming with her, and thus kept her from rolling. Embarrassed beyond belief, she finally gave up. "Yes. I do need help. But close your eyes, for heaven's sake."

He chuckled. "If I close my eyes, I won't be able to untangle you."

"Can you at least slide the curtain rod out of the loops?"

He leaned over her and disassembled the end of the rod, easily sliding it free of the loops. Setting it aside, he reached out to her. "Take my hand."

"No, I'm not dressed."

"Auntie Lily, are you all right?" Robbie asked from the door to the bathroom.

"I'm fine," Lily called out. "I just slipped. I'll be out in a minute. Please keep watch on Mari."

"Okay." Robbie turned back to the room and his Lego tower he'd been building.

She struggled to right herself but couldn't. "Don't just stand there, do something."

He bent, took her hand and hauled Lily to her feet all in one powerful motion. He pulled so fast she didn't have time to get her feet firmly planted. She went from lying on the floor to crashing into his chest.

Tony wrapped his arms around her waist to steady her.

The shower curtain had slipped down below her breasts, and the towel was somewhere between her belly and his hips.

When he started to lean back, she leaned into him. "Don't."

"Don't what?"

"Don't move." She stared at his Adam's apple, her cheeks on fire. "I'm naked."

He chuckled, again. "I hope you are, since you were in the shower."

"I mean, the shower curtain slipped down," she whispered.

His laughter rumbled in his chest, resonating through hers. Her body quivered, and heat coiled low in her belly. Why did he have such a visceral effect on her?

Because he was drop-dead gorgeous. Because his hands were on her naked body. Well, on the shower curtain around her naked body. And what was that hard ridge pressing into her belly?

Lily gulped. Could he be as aware of her, as she was of him?

"It's not funny," she whispered. "What will the children think with you holding me and me… well…naked?"

"They'll think I helped you when you fell in the bathroom." His mouth was so close to her temple, she could feel the warmth of his breath on her skin.

Desperate to get away from the man before she did something even stupider, like throw her arms around him and beg him to take her to bed, she asked, "How am I supposed to bow out of this situation gracefully?"

He tipped her chin up to stare down into her eyes. "Hmm. You are in a bind, aren't you?"

"You're no help." With her hands against his shirt, she dug her fingers and thumbs into his shirt and pinched him.

"Ouch!" He jerked back. "Why'd you do that?"

She tightened her hold around him. "You're not taking me seriously."

"Hey, I got you off the floor," he reminded her. "And I should get some credit for saving you from the killer curtain rod."

"Okay, so you're not all bad," Lily admitted. "I still don't know how I'm going to get dressed without exposing myself to you and those sweet children."

He reached behind her, grabbed another towel from the towel bar and draped it over her shoulders. "There. Don't say I can't be helpful."

She pulled the edges of the towel around her like a sarong, letting the shower curtain drop to the floor. Once she had all the important parts covered, she stepped out of Tony's arms. "I can take it from here. Thank you."

He touched the tips of two fingers to his brow. "Glad to be off assistance." He backed out of the bathroom and pulled the door closed.

Alone at last, Lily stared at the door, her pulse racing, her body on fire from touching his. If there hadn't been children in the other room… Holy crap, she'd wanted to let that shower curtain fall to the ground, *without* the towel.

This was not good. Not good at all. The idea behind being an au pair was to care for the children, not fall for the parent.

CHAPTER 6

TONY CHECKED on Robbie and Mari, and then crossed the living room to the other bedroom in the suite. He found himself in need of a very cold shower. Holding the naked au pair had stirred responses he hadn't felt since Marisol had passed.

What was it about the pretty teacher that had his body tense and his manhood rock-hard? She was just a stubborn, opinionated woman who happened to be good with children. He wasn't in Costa Rica to have a fling. Especially since his children were sharing the same space with him and Lily.

And Lily was his employee. Tony did not have relationships with anyone who worked for him. It wasn't right, and it caused far too many complications.

And Lily Grayson had complication written all over her pretty face.

But when she'd wrapped her arms around his waist and pressed her wet, naked breasts against his chest, any self-imposed rules he'd lived by for so long flew out the window. He'd wanted to close the door, strip off his clothes and have her against the tile walls of the shower.

His lips twitched thinking about what her response would have been. She'd either have joined willingly or slammed him face-down on the floor, like she'd done with Michael's dad.

The woman had mad skills when it came to self-defense.

Tony stripped out of the clothes he'd worn all day to travel in. A moment later, he was under the shower's spray, rinsing off the germs and grime from traveling so far in one day. The chilled water went a long way toward returning control of his body to his heart and mind.

Sanity restored, he dried his body and dressed in tailored black trousers, a white dress shirt and patent leather loafers. When he stepped out of his room, he came to a full stop, his gaze taking in the beauty in front of him.

Lily wore an emerald green gown that matched the color of her eyes. The soft material hugged her body like a second skin, the thin straps accentuating the curves of her shoulders. She'd dried her hair and pulled it up into a messy bun on top of her head, with wispy strands curling around her ears.

Robbie emerged from the room dressed in a pair of trousers and a crisp white shirt, much like the one Tony wore. His brown hair had been neatly combed back from his face.

Mari ran out of the room dressed in a ruffled white dress with a big bow tied in the back. Her hair had been pulled up into a messy bun, much like Lily's.

Tony's heart swelled at how beautiful his children were. "You've performed a miracle. I could never have achieved such perfection."

She smiled as Robbie and Mari came to stand beside her. "They wanted to look good for you."

He gave them a slight bow. "I am honored."

"I look like you, Papi." Robbie's chest puffed out, so proud to be a man like his father.

"Yes, son, you do." Though he resembled his mother more, Tony kept that thought to himself. "Ready?"

Lily hesitated. "I wasn't sure if you wanted me to accompany your family to dinner."

"You have to eat too, don't you? Or are you one of those women who doesn't eat to spare her figure?"

Lily snorted. "Obviously, I like to eat."

He tilted his head, his gaze sweeping her from head to toe. "Not so obvious. Are you coming? Robbie and Mari seem to like you. They'll be disappointed if you don't come."

Lily cocked an auburn brow. "And you?"

His lips quirked as he fought a smile. "My opinion isn't as important."

"I wouldn't be here, if that were true," she pointed out.

"Well said." He held out his arm to Lily. "It would be my pleasure to escort such a lovely lady to dinner with my children."

"You don't have to lay it on so thick." She slipped her hand into the crook of his elbow. "A simple *you can come* would have sufficed." Giving him a sideways glance, she added, "But thank you."

They rode the elevator to the second floor where the restaurant was located. Robbie and Mari gave him a rundown of their fun in the pool and how well they could swim.

At the restaurant, they were given a table by a window with a view of the ocean. The sun had settled like a big orange ball on the horizon, sinking into the water and spreading fire across its surface.

"Beautiful," Lily murmured.

Tony couldn't agree more. The little teacher from Hellfire, Texas was bathed in the glow of a brilliant sunset, the fiery highlights in her auburn hair burned brightly. With her hair pinned up on top of her head, her delicate earlobes were exposed, as well as the long smooth line of her neck.

A waitress hurried over to take their drink orders, forcing Tony to shift his attention from the lovely au pair to a member of his staff, eager to please.

Sharing a meal with Lily and his children was an unexpected joy. Robbie and Mari were at their best. Lily was attentive and helpful with their wants and needs. She was patient, kind and always had a smile for the little ones.

Tony found himself wishing she would turn her smile in his direction. Perhaps he had to earn her pleasure. The thought of earning her approval irritated him at the same time as it challenged him.

After dinner, they took the children up to the room where Lily helped them into their pajamas, got them to brush their teeth and tucked them into one of the double beds.

Still wearing her pretty green dress, she kicked off her shoes, sat on the edge of Mari's mattress and read a book, pointing to the pictures and asking Mari and Robbie to name the animals in the story. In English.

Tony stood in the doorway, listening to the sweet sound of Lily's voice as she told the story of a lost lamb finding her way back to her mother. When she finished the book, Mari's eyes had closed, and her breathing had deepened. Lily rose from the bed, slid Mari over onto a pillow and kissed her goodnight.

Robbie slipped out of the bed and rubbed his eyes "What if the lamb's mother had died?"

The question tore at Tony's heart. He held his breath, waiting for Lily's response.

She slipped an arm around his shoulders and hugged him close, dropping a kiss on top of his head.

"Then her father would find her and love her even more."

Tony entered the room, lifted his son into his arms and held him close. "That's right. Her father would have found her and loved her enough for both parents." He laid Robbie in his bed and drew the blanket up under his chin. "Just like I love you and Mari so very much."

Robbie wrapped his arms around Tony's neck and pulled him close. "I love you, Papi," he whispered. "Please don't go away like Mama."

"I won't," he said.

"Papi?" Robbie said as he loosened his hold and sank back against the pillow. "My friend Michael is getting a new daddy. Can we get a new mama?"

Tony smiled down at his son. "I don't know. That's a big order to fill. I'd have to find a nice lady I can love as much as I loved your mama. And she'd have to love me and you and Mari."

Robbie sighed. "Auntie Lily loves us. Don't you?" He turned to Lily who had been picking up discarded clothing and folding them neatly.

She blinked. "Of course, I do."

"Then all you have to do is fall in love with my papi, and you can be my mama."

Lily's cheeks flooded with color. "It's not that simple, Robbie."

"Why not?" he asked.

"It's just not," Tony responded. "Go to sleep now.

I'm sure Miss Grayson has lots of fun things planned for you tomorrow."

"Are we going to the beach?" Robbie asked.

"I think that's a good idea," Lily said.

"If I can get away, I'll come with you," Tony said, hoping he wasn't making a promise he couldn't keep.

"Good, then you and Auntie Lily could work on falling in love." Robbie turned over and tucked his hand beneath his cheek, a smile on his face as he closed his eyes.

Tony leaned down and pressed a kiss to his son's forehead. "*Buenas noches. Te amo hijo.*"

"*Yo te quiero más,*" Robbie mumbled.

Lily gathered her nightclothes and started for the bathroom.

"I had the staff fix the shower curtain while we were at dinner," Tony said.

"Thank you. I'm sorry I destroyed the one that was there."

"I'm not."

She shot him a wide-eyed glance, her lovely green eyes making him want so much more.

The things he was feeling threatened to overwhelm him. "Goodnight, Lily," he said, and he walked away before he said or did anything else that didn't make any sense.

Lily remained awake long after she changed into

her nightgown and lay on the small bed that had been brought into the living room, complete with sheets, blankets and extra pillows.

What had Tony meant when he'd said that he wasn't sorry she'd destroyed the shower curtain?

Had he felt something when she'd been pressed up against him naked? More than just embarrassment at having an employee standing naked with him in the same room?

Her heart fluttered, skipped several beats and pounded against her ribs.

Antonio Delossantos was a very handsome man. He could have his pick of any woman. Why would he pick a teacher from Texas?

Lily punched her pillow and turned on her side. No, she was reading too much into what he'd said. Besides, she was an employee, there to take care of his children, not him. When the summer was over, she wouldn't see him again. Robbie would be in a first-grade class, and Mari would likely have a different kindergarten teacher.

Closing her eyes, Lily focused on the next day and the activities she had planned for Robbie and Mari. They would go to the beach and maybe do a little shopping in the market. Lily also wanted to work with Robbie and Mari on reading skills to prepare them for the next school year. She would make it fun, so they wouldn't even think it was work.

She woke the next morning determined to keep

her head on straight, enjoy her time in Costa Rica and the children she was coming to care for dearly.

What woman wouldn't fall in love with Robbie and Mari? They were sweet, full of energy and happy, for the most part. Robbie had his moments when he missed his mother. But Mari had been too young to remember her.

Lily packed a large bag full of beach towels, water bottles and sunscreen. After breakfast, Tony headed for his office, promising to join them when he got free. Lily took the children up to their suite where she helped Mari and Robbie into their swimsuits. Then she dressed in her bikini and pulled a light summer dress over the suit.

The three walked through the hotel and out to the beach where they claimed an umbrella and a few lounge chairs to drop their things on. Then they waded out into the surf. Mari was more reluctant than Robbie. The beach was beautiful, and the water was clear and clean. Costa Rica was a paradise Lily could easily fall in love with.

For all its beauty, the country had a dark side. From what Tony had told Lily, his wife had been murdered by a member of a drug cartel.

Lily could understand Tony's reticence in bringing his children back to a place where the local police had little control over the drug traffickers. That he had chosen her to watch over them showed how much he trusted her abilities.

She was holding Mari's hands as she jumped a wave when Tony joined them, wearing a pair of black swim trunks and nothing else.

Lily's breath caught in her chest.

The man had broad shoulders, muscular arms and taut abs. As he walked toward her, Lily could barely form a coherent thought.

He smiled and held out his arms. "Want me to take her?"

Her knees wobbled, and she had to think to process his words. "No. I've got her. Right, Mari?"

Mari giggled and kicked at the waves.

Tony scooped Robbie up and tossed him into the water.

Robbie came up smiling. "Do it again, Papi."

The two guys splashed and played while Lily and Mari sat in the sand, letting the waves wash over their legs.

When the sun got too hot, they moved to the shade of the umbrella and drank from the water bottles.

A man dressed in the uniform of the hotel staff brought out sack lunches for them, and they enjoyed a picnic on the beach.

When Mari fell asleep on one of the lounge chairs, Lily repacked their bag, slipped into her dress and stood.

Tony carried Mari, and Lily followed, holding onto Robbie's hand.

Lily couldn't help feeling like they'd spent the day as a family. If she were married and had children, she would hope they would be as happy as they had all seemed to be that day.

TONY HAD HURRIED through his morning meeting with the staff and read through the status and financial reports. Nothing stood out that needed immediate attention, so he'd changed into his swimsuit and joined Lily and the kids at the beach.

It had been a long time since he'd enjoyed a day so much. It made him realize just how distant he'd been with Robbie and Mari. He'd left raising his children to Rosa, when they'd needed him most. Now that he could see what he'd done, he regretted missing so much time he could have spent getting to know his children better

Lily had helped him to see what he'd been missing. She'd done it from the moment she'd told him off in front of the school, to the way she showered his children with the kind of love and support they truly deserved.

Being on the beach had brought back memories of spending time with his parents on that very strip of sand, when he was Robbie's age. They'd been there for him every step of the way. Robbie and Mari deserved no less.

He'd wallowed in his grief long enough. It was

time to get on with living and being a part of his children's lives.

When they entered the lobby of the hotel, he spotted Marcus and waved him over.

Lily held out her arms. "Let me hold her."

Tony transferred his daughter into Lily's hands, and then turned to Marcus. "Do you have a fishing trip scheduled for tomorrow?"

Marcus shook his head. "I have a sightseeing boat trip scheduled. Is there something you'd like me to do?"

"I'd like you to take me, Robbie, Mari and Lily fishing and snorkeling."

"How about the day after tomorrow? I don't have anything scheduled then," Marcus offered.

Robbie's eyes widened. "We get to go fishing and snorkeling?" He looked up at Lily, a grin spreading across his face. "Did you hear that?"

Lily frowned. "Are you sure Mari's big enough to go along?"

"We'll take special care of her," Marcus assured her. "I have a life vest that will fit her perfectly."

"What do you say?" Tony asked, glancing down at Robbie. "Do you want to see some fish, and then catch some?"

"Yes!" Robbie yelled.

At the sound of Robbie's excitement, Mari lifted her head and blinked open her eyes.

"What about you?" Tony directed his question to Lily. "Are you up for a boat ride?"

She nodded. "Sounds like fun."

"Good, then it's all settled." Tony turned to Marcus. "Eight at the dock, the day after tomorrow?"

Marcus grinned. "Great. I'll have the boat ready. My deckhands will be glad for another day's wages." Marcus shot a glance toward Lily and the children. "Can we talk in private?"

"I'll be right back," Tony excused himself and stepped aside with Marcus. "What's up?"

"I've had some of my security guards quit today."

Tony frowned. "How many?"

"Almost half. Some didn't show up for work this morning. When I called the others, they informed me they no longer wished to work at the Bahía Azul."

Tony's frown deepened. "Did they say why?"

Marcus shook his head. "I tried to find out through the grapevine, but no one's talking."

"Can you hire more?"

Marcus shook his head. "I hesitate to hire local. Until I find out the cause of the sudden exodus, I don't trust that those I hire will stick around. Nor will they be up to speed on what it takes to be a security guard here."

"Do you have any suggestions in the meantime?"

Marcus nodded. "I've been in touch with a former teammate of mine from when I was in the Navy. He's started a security service up in Montana, employing prior special operations men who've come off active duty. They're combat trained and highly skilled. It might cost you more, but if they say they'll be here, they'll be here."

Tony's jaw tightened. "Get them. Until we know what's going on, I prefer to have people we can depend on. The safety of our clientele and staff is what's important."

"He said he could fly four men in by morning."

"Good." He touched Marcus's arm. "As soon as you hear anything about why the guards quit, let me know."

Tony turned back to Lily and the children. Their smiles helped lift his spirits after Marcus's disturbing news.

Robbie skipped all the way to the elevator, chattering on about the big fish he would catch.

His excitement was contagious, making Tony look forward to their fishing adventure.

"I'll have to work this afternoon and much of tomorrow to free up the following morning for fishing." He handed Lily a credit card. "You'll want to do some shopping to find them snorkels and masks. The boat has some, but a thousand tourists have used them."

"What about fishing poles?" she asked.

"Marcus has the best. He'll have what we need in the way of bait and tackle." Tony nodded toward one of the valets. "Juan can drive you into town tomorrow and show you the best place to find what you're looking for."

The valet hurried over. Tony told him what he wanted, speaking in Spanish.

When Tony was done, Juan grinned at Lily. "I'll take you where you want to go. When would you like to leave?"

Lily hefted Mari in her arms. "Tomorrow, an hour before noon…? Then we can have lunch in town."

Juan nodded. "I'll be here when you're ready. Just come to the lobby and ask the concierge for me."

Tony took Mari from Lily and carried her all the way up to the penthouse where he laid her on the bed.

Mari sat up and rubbed her eyes. When she tried to get off the bed, Lily laid down with her on one side and Robbie on the other.

"Go on to work," Lily said, waving him away. "We'll be fine after a little nap."

Tony would rather have stayed and joined them.

Robbie leaned his cheek against Lily's shoulder, while Mari curled her tiny body into her au pair.

He could have stood there all day, loving how the three of them looked all snuggled together, but Tony had work to do.

With his children and their au pair to come back to, he made sure he didn't bury himself in the work he did. In the short time he'd known Lily Grayson, he'd learned so much about her, Robbie and Mari.

Most of all, he'd learned about himself. Life was short. Marisol's death had taught him that. The little teacher from Hellfire had taught him he couldn't waste a second of precious time with his family. Along with this golden nugget of insight, he realized Lily was becoming more and more a part of his family.

CHAPTER 7

FISHING DAY dawned bright and beautifully clear, with the sun warming the sky and a gentle ocean breeze making the air fresh and slightly salty.

Lily stretched and smiled. She was surprised Robbie and Mari hadn't already climbed out of bed and come to crawl into her little rollaway. The sun was just edging its way around the blinds, making the room lighter.

Lily had taken the children shopping for masks and snorkels the day before and had lunch at a cute little café overlooking the waterfront. The children had behaved beautifully and, as a treat, she'd bought them ice cream. After a short nap back at the hotel, Lily had taken them out to the pool and let them play for an hour.

At dinner that night, Robbie couldn't stop talking

about the day they'd spent at the market, and Mari had shared with her father the English words for the food she ate. All in all, the day couldn't have been finer.

Unless Tony could have spent more time with them. At least they had him for breakfast and dinner. Lily looked forward to those hours, sitting across the table from him, her heart beating a little faster, and her face heating every time he glanced her way.

The man appeared more relaxed. Happier.

Lily glanced at the clock. They had exactly one and a half hours to dress, eat and get down to the boat. She threw back the blanket, rose from her bed and opened the blinds to the sunshine.

"About time someone woke up," a deep voice said from across the room.

Lily spun to face Tony, already dressed in shorts, a loose light blue guayabera shirt and deck shoes. He'd shaved and combed his thick black hair back, though one strand always managed to fall forward over his forehead, as if in protest. The manmade casual look amazing.

Lily's breath caught and held before she found her tongue. "Good morning." Then she realized she was still wearing her not-so-sexy flamingo pajamas, and she probably had bed hair. She raised her hand to smooth the tangles. "I'll get the children up and dressed."

"No hurry. We still have plenty of time. Can I offer you a cup of coffee or tea?" He waived to the mini kitchen in the apartment.

"Tea would be nice. But I can get it. Have you had your coffee yet?" She laughed. "Of course, you haven't. I've been out here snoozing while you've patiently waited. How long have you been up?"

"About an hour."

Her eyebrows shot up. "That long? You should have gotten me up. I guess it's awkward me sleeping out here. You could have enjoyed a cup of coffee while relaxing on the sofa and enjoying the view."

He turned to fill the carafe with water at the sink in the mini bar and poured it into the coffee maker. "I didn't mind waiting on the coffee. And I was relaxing on the sofa, enjoying the view." With the water poured, he turned, his lips curved upward at the corners. "Did you know that you talk in your sleep?"

Lily pressed a hand to her mouth. "I do?"

"Oh, it's not loud, and I couldn't make out what you were saying, but yes, you do."

She frowned. "You were watching me?"

"Not so much watching. I was reading the paper, listening to you mumble."

Her cheeks heated. "Maybe I could move the bed into the room with the children, so that I don't disturb your morning routine. You should have woken me."

"No, please. I found the sound strangely soothing. I was afraid I'd wake you by rattling my paper."

"I'm so sorry. An au pair should be almost invisible. Only showing up when the client needs her." She straightened the sheets and blankets on the bed and fluffed the pillow. "Really, we should ask them to move the bed into the other room. I can sleep in there."

"You worry too much. I only made an observation. The sleeping arrangements are fine the way they are."

"If you're sure... I guess I should get dressed and wake the children." She started for the bedroom door.

"Please, let them sleep a little longer. I love their enthusiasm in the morning, but it's also nice to sit in the quiet and enjoy the sun rising over the ocean." He poured hot water into a ceramic mug and dropped a tea bag into it. "What do you like in your tea?"

"I'll fix it while you make your coffee." Feeling a little self-conscious in her flamingo pajamas, she joined him at the bar, mixed a little sugar into her mug and removed the teabag. Standing so close to him that early in the morning made her nervous. Especially since he was dressed for the day, and she was still in her pajamas. She glanced up at the mirror over the bar and gasped at her reflection. "Oh, my. I look like something the cat dragged in."

"You look lovely."

"With my hair sticking out like a wicked witch's?" She finger-combed her hair, trying to smooth out the tangles.

Tony captured her hand. "Let me." He weaved his fingers through her hair, gently easing tangles free. When he was finished, he stared into the mirror from behind her. "Better?"

She nodded, her heart pounding and her body on fire from his nearness. "You do that so well."

"I do this for Mari when she doesn't want me to brush her hair."

Tony poured his coffee into a mug and waved toward the sofa. "We have maybe five minutes, if we're lucky, before they wake."

Lily took her tea and sat on one end of the sofa, facing the view of the ocean. She tucked her legs under her and sipped her tea, the warmth of it nice after the coolness of the air-conditioned room. "You must love coming here. It's so beautiful."

"It has its beauty, and its ugly side." He stared out at the ocean, as if looking into the past.

"What do you mean?"

"Of course, the land, the sea and the sunsets are beyond compare. But Costa Rica has its problems. Being halfway between the source of drugs and the consumers, it has become a warehouse of sorts for storing the product in transit."

"Are the drug cartels here like the ones in Mexico?" Lily asked.

He nodded. "They work as an extension of the cartels in Mexico. The murder rate in Costa Rica has risen over the past decade. Most of those murders have been drug-related crimes."

Lily looked over the rim of her mug at him. "Is that what happened to your wife?"

Tony drew in a deep breath and let it out slowly before answering. "Marisol was visiting a friend's mother who was sick. The woman lived in a poor barrio on the south side of the town. When she left the house, she happened to step out at the same time as a drug lord was performing a hit on a group of men who'd crossed him. Marisol was caught in the crossfire."

Lily's heart pinched hard in her chest at the anger and sadness in Tony's words.

"She'd asked me to take her there, but I was too busy handling some insignificant employee crisis at the time. If I had gone…" His words faded off as he stared out at the ocean.

"You can't second-guess the past. If you had gone, most likely, you'd have been killed as well. Then Robbie and Mari would have been parentless. Who would have raised them?"

Tony shook his head. "Marisol's parents died in a motor vehicle accident. Mine had me when they were older. They passed shortly after Mari was born."

"Don't you see?" Lily leaned forward. "Had you gone with Marisol, your children would have been orphans. They need a parent to be there for them. They need you."

Tony's gaze shifted from the ocean back to Lily. "They needed their mother. She was so much better at parenting than I've been."

"Don't knock yourself," she said. "You're not doing such a bad job."

Tony snorted. "That's not what you told me on Robbie's last day of school." His lips twisted into a wry grin.

"Well, maybe I was a little harsh." She sat back with her mug of tea. "Besides, it's never too late to work on being a good parent. You're making good progress, from what I can tell."

He tilted his head, one eyebrow hiking. "I'm glad I've met with your approval."

She shook her head. "You don't need my approval. You need the approval and trust of Robbie and Mari." She smiled as she recalled their day at the beach. "They really do love you."

"Is today fishing day?" Robbie emerged from the bedroom rubbing his sleepy eyes.

Tony held open his arms. "Yes, it is."

Robbie ran into his father's embrace and snuggled against him.

Mari toddled out next, yawning and holding a

pink teddy bear by the arm. When she saw Robbie in Tony's arms, she turned and ran toward Lily.

Lily set her mug on the end table and lifted the little girl onto her lap.

Mari leaned her cheek against Lily's breast and closed her eyes. "*Te amo*."

Lily's heart swelled, and she whispered, "I love you, too."

"I love you, too," Mari echoed, followed quickly by, "I'm hungry."

Lily's smile broadened. Mari had continued with a new thought…in English. Without being prompted. Between the nightly reading and working with her all day, the little girl was improving quite well. At the rate she was going, she'd be ready for kindergarten and bilingual to boot. Lily didn't want to discourage her from speaking both languages. She actually believed learning different languages should begin at an early age, when a child's mind was like a sponge.

"Let's get you dressed," Lily said, "and we'll go down for breakfast."

"How about we order room service?" Tony lifted the phone on the table beside him. "It will be here by the time you're ready." He quickly placed the order and added an order for lunches to take with them on their boating adventure.

Lily gathered the children and herded them toward their bedroom where they chose outfits that they didn't mind getting dirty. She dressed Mari in a two-piece swimsuit with a bright pink shirt and a pair of matching shorts. Robbie wore his superhero swim trunks and a matching royal blue superhero T-shirt with all his favorite heroes displayed.

Tony appeared in the doorway. "I'll do Mari's hair while you get ready."

Lily handed him the brush and elastic band. "I was going to put her hair in two braids so that she could wear a hat to shade her face." She grinned, grabbed her swimsuit, shorts and a T-shirt and headed for the bathroom. "You do know how to braid, don't you?"

"Sure," Tony said, frowning down at Mari's hair.

Lily was still smiling as she stripped out of her pajamas and stood naked in front of the mirror. Her cheeks were flushed, and she looked happier than she'd felt in a long time. The thought of Tony on the other side of the door made heat coil at her core. What would he do if she asked him to braid her hair? Now...while she was completely naked?

Lily shook her head. That would never happen. Not when two small children were in the other room, unsupervised.

She'd chosen to wear her bikini with a T-shirt and shorts over them. It didn't take long for her to dress and brush her hair. She pulled it all back and braided it into one thick plait hanging down her back. It wouldn't behave for long in the wind and humidity, but it would do for a start. Packing sunscreen, towels and a brush into a beach bag, she finally came out of the bathroom.

A member of the hotel staff was pushing a rolling cart through the door laden with covered dishes, glasses of orange juice and chocolate milk.

The four of them sat at the small table and dug into the meal, laughing and talking about the fish they hoped to catch.

When they were finished and had brushed their teeth, they hurried down to the lobby and the SUV that would take them to the dock where they'd meet Marcus. The drive to the dock took only minutes.

Lily carried the beach bag with the towels, snorkeling gear and sunscreen, while Tony carried the ice chest packed with their lunches. Robbie ran ahead. Lily held tightly to Mari's hand to keep her from following her brother.

Marcus stood on the dock to welcome his passengers to the Lost Cause. While Tony and Lily stepped onto the boat, Marcus helped the little ones into life vests before they were allowed on board. Two deckhands worked around the passengers, cutting bait and preparing the fishing rods.

Minutes later, Marcus maneuvered the boat away from the dock and out into the open water.

Lily stood with Robbie and Mari at the bow,

letting the wind blow through her hair, the salty spray kicking up around her.

“Have you been deep sea fishing before?” Tony asked, coming to stand beside them.

“I have. I love the feel of the salty wind against my skin and the sound of the seagulls calling out overhead.”

“Marcus knows the best places to catch the big fish,” Tony said.

“Hopefully, he knows places to catch smaller ones as well.” Lily smiled down at Mari. “I don’t want these little guys to be yanked out of the boat by a whopping big swordfish.”

Tony grinned. “They’d lose grip on the rod before they’d be yanked out of the boat. But I agree. We don’t want to take chances.”

After traveling for thirty minutes, Marcus slowed the craft and brought it to a halt. He climbed down from his high perch at the helm and clapped his hands together. “Let’s fish!”

Marcus and the deckhands equipped them with fishing poles and bait, and then showed them how to let the line loose until it went slack. They gave Robbie and Mari smaller poles they could handle with their little hands and lowered the lines into the water for them.

No sooner had they dropped their lines to the bottom then the fish took the bait and swam with it.

“I’ve got one!” Robbie cried, excitedly. He turned

the handle on the reel as fast as he could. The little pole bent over, the fish on the hook giving a good fight.

One of the deckhands stood by with a fishnet, waiting to step in should Robbie need help. The little boy cranked the handle on the reel, working feverishly to bring in the feisty fish.

"You've got it, Robbie. Stay with him," Tony called out. A tug on his own line made him focus on what he had in his hands.

Lily laughed, enjoying the excitement of the moment.

Marcus squatted behind Mari, his arms around her, helping her hold her rod, showing her how to turn the reel. When a fish bit her hook, Marcus helped her jerk back the rod, setting the hook. Then he helped her reel in the fish, alternating between her turning the handle and him.

Robbie, with the help of the Costa Rican teenaged deckhand, brought his fish up close enough to the surface the deckhand could scoop it up in the net. He identified it as a snapper.

"Look, Papi! It's a ginormous snapper!" The deckhand hung it on a peg and stood Robbie beside it to get a photograph of the boy and his fish. Robbie raced back to his rod and waited impatiently for the deckhand to bait his hook again.

Meanwhile, Mari let Marcus reel her fish all the way to the surface. When they brought it out of the water, it slipped free and flopped on the deck. Mari squealed and squeezed her eyes shut.

"Is Mari doing okay?" Tony asked as he leaned back with his pole, creating a little slack, then he reeled as fast as he could, before leaning back again.

"She's doing great. She just landed another snapper," Marcus said. "Gio's going to help her get her line back in the water." He moved over to help Lily.

"I can manage on my own," Lily said.

"Yeah, but you won't catch much if your bait's gone." He took the rod from her and reeled it in. The hook was bare.

Lily propped her fists on the hips "Why those little sneaks."

"Why don't you move to the bow? There's less competition up there." He carried her rod and a small bucket of bait.

Lily followed, looking back at the children. "I'm not sure I want to be this far away from Robbie and Mari. What if they fall in?"

"They have three people watching them closely. A fourth will be overkill. Besides, you have to catch a fish just like the others. You can't let a four-year-old catch a fish and you come up empty-handed."

"I'm okay. I don't have to catch a fish to be happy." She stood by while Marcus baited the hook, loosened the reel and dropped the hook into the water.

"When it goes slack—"

"I know," she said, rolling her eyes. "Turn the reel

a couple times to bring it off the bottom." She gave him a mock salute. "Aye, aye, captain."

Though he didn't give her anymore fishing advice, Marcus remained on the deck of the bow with her. He leaned his back against the wheelhouse and crossed his arms over his chest. "What are your intentions toward the boss?" he asked.

Caught completely off balance, Lily let go of the handle on the reel. At that moment, a fish hit her line and practically ripped the rod out of her hand. She fought to get it under control, using the time it took to come up with a response to Marcus's question.

She chose evasion as her method. "I don't know what you're talking about."

"I see the way you look at him," Marcus said softly. "And I see the way he looks at you. Something's going on."

Heat rushed into Lily's cheeks. "Nothing's going on," she said. It wasn't as if they'd kissed or anything. She had been almost naked in his company, but that had been an accident. "Why do you ask?"

"I've known Tony, going on five years. I knew him when Robbie was just a baby, and Marisol was pregnant with Mari." He paused. "He took her death hard. I don't want to see him hurt."

Lily frowned. "You think I would hurt him?" She shook her head. "I'm here to care for the children. I'm just an employee."

Marcus chuckled. "Sweetheart, you're more than that."

Frowning, she tilted her head. "What is Tony to you? I thought you worked for him."

"He's my friend. I work with him, helping him with security for his hotel. He helped me out of a dark place in my life and gave me the loan to buy my boat. I've since paid him back, but I will never forget how good he has been to me and to others. The man deserves happiness in his life."

"He's got two beautiful children," Lily said. "That should go a long way toward his happiness."

"It does." Marcus pointed to the rod. "The hook has reached the bottom. You need to give it a couple good turns to bring it up a bit."

Lily did and immediately felt a tug. She jerked back on the rod to set the hook and felt another tug. "I've got one," she said, glad for the activity that would keep Marcus from asking anymore questions about her intentions toward her boss.

She had no intentions. The man was clearly way out of her league. He was wealthy, incredibly handsome and could have his pick of any woman. What would he find at all interesting in her?

Nothing.

She was just the au pair, watching out for his children. A poor teacher from Texas. Nothing at all exciting about that.

Lily reeled in the fish, bringing it to the surface.

Marcus whistled. "You've caught a nice sized dorado. That's good eating, if you're into Mahi-Mahi." Marcus scooped it out of the water into a net and carried it to the back of the boat.

Lily followed.

Tony was still working on bringing in his fish, his rod bent in half, his face strained and sweat popping out on his brow. "Remind me to work out more often. This guy is giving me a run for my money."

"Want me to take him for a while?" Marcus asked, coming up behind him.

"No, I've got it," Tony said through gritted teeth.

When Marcus offered to bait Lily's hook again, she shook her head. "I'm waiting to see what Tony's got. It has to be big."

For the next twenty minutes, Tony fought the fish, slowly but steadily bringing it in. When it came within a yard of the boat, Marcus snagged it with a hook on the end of a pole and dragged it up onto the deck. "Yellowfin tuna," he announced. "I'm betting it's at least eighty pounds. Nice."

Robbie and Mari's eyes rounded.

Lily laughed. "It's bigger than Robbie and Mari put together."

"No wonder it was such a challenge to bring in." Tony flexed his muscles and rubbed his shoulders. "I could use a break. Anyone up for lunch?"

Robbie and Mari both yelled, "Yes!"

Lily washed her hands and helped Mari and Robbie wash theirs, too.

Soon they were sitting in the cabin, with the door open to the breeze, sharing their lunch with Marcus and the deckhands, talking about how they brought in their catches and what they would be having for dinner that night.

By the time they finished, it was getting hot. They decided it was time to test their snorkeling gear.

Marcus drove the boat over to a protected cove with a sandy beach and water so clear they could see thirty feet down.

Lily slathered sunscreen on Robbie and Mari and started to put it on herself when Tony took over and got the spots she missed on her back and shoulders. Her heart turned flips, and her pulse hammered the entire time his hands slid across her skin, evoking all kinds of naughty thoughts she shouldn't be having about her boss. When he was done, Lily couldn't get into the water fast enough to cool her heated senses.

They spent the next hour snorkeling and walking along the beach, picking up shells. By the time Mari asked to be held and laid her head on Lily's shoulder, Lily was ready to call it a day and head back.

The day had been magical. Her time spent with Tony and the kids would forever be a fond memory. Lily began to dread the day they'd head back to Hellfire and leave all this behind.

On the way back to the dock, Lily laid Mari on a

padded bench in the cabin with her little head in Lily's lap. Robbie sat beside her, leaning against her arm, his eyes drooping.

Lily could relate. She could easily fall asleep as the boat plowed through the water, gently rocking them all.

Tony had gone up to the helm where Marcus steered the boat. After a while, he came down to check on them.

As he stared at her and his children, all thoughts of sleep left Lily's mind. The electric current between them practically sparkled.

"Lily, what is it about you that makes me want…" He stopped, as if searching for the right word.

Lily held her breath and waited for him to find it.

He opened his mouth to continue but was cut off when the boat jerked to the right.

Lily barely managed to keep the children from falling off the bench. "What the heck?" she muttered and tightened her hold around Mari and Robbie.

Tony staggered, righted himself and worked his way to the door.

A deckhand dropped down from the helm where Marcus stood, his eyes wide. "Mr. Marcus wants us all to stay in the cabin and get down on the floor." He hurried out to the other deckhand, who had been busy stowing the fishing equipment, and pulled him into the cabin.

Tony helped Lily pull the cushion off the seat and

settle it on the floor. Mari blinked a couple times but was too sleepy to wake.

Robbie clung to Lily's hand. "Why are we sitting on the floor?"

Lily pulled him close and held onto him and Mari. "I don't know." She looked up at Tony.

Tony's steady gaze held hers for a moment. "I'm going to find out."

CHAPTER 8

As Tony climbed up the ladder to the helm, he looked out over the water and spotted another boat, turning around and heading back toward them. The boat wasn't a pleasure boat, but one like the Navy SEALs might use on a commando raid.

His pulse leaping, Tony scrambled up the rest of the way to the top where Marcus stood cursing.

"What's happening?" Tony demanded.

"That boat tried to ram us," he said. "I was able to turn in time to miss them, but they're coming back at us." His jaw tightened, and his lips thinned. "And it looks like they have guns." Marcus handed Tony a set of binoculars.

Tony lifted them to his eyes, focused on the oncoming boat and swore. "*Madre de Dios!*"

"They're aiming for us," Marcus said. "You might want to get down in the cabin and stay low."

"I can't leave you up here, exposed to the gunfire." He jerked his thumb. "Go below. Now."

"Can't let you do that, boss." Marcus shook his head. "You need to get down there and protect those kids of yours. I don't have anyone depending on me. You do."

"That doesn't make your life any less important," Tony argued.

"It does in my mind. Please," he tossed over his shoulder. "They're coming in range, and I need to perform some evasive maneuvers. I can't do that with you hanging onto the ladder. Go!"

"Do you have any guns on board?"

"There's a rifle in the cabinet over the scuba gear. You have to dig to the back. The rounds are in the pink fishing tackle box beside it."

Tony scrambled down the ladder and dove into the cabin.

"What's happening?" Lily asked.

Tony didn't want to say anything to frighten the children. "There's a situation. We're handling it. The best thing you can do is keep yourself and the children as low as possible." He turned to the deckhands and repeated the instructions in Spanish.

The young men nodded and hunkered low on the floor.

While Mari slept and Robbie clutched Lily's arm, Tony dug through the cabinet over the scuba gear until his hand closed around the rifle hidden at the back. He found the pink tackle box and pulled out a box of bullets. When he brought the rifle out of the cabinet, a collective gasp sounded from the deckhands and Lily.

"Just how bad is the situation?" Lily asked, her face pale and her eyes wide and worried.

"Marcus is working on outrunning it." He tilted his head toward the rifle. "This is just in case."

"Do you know how to use it?" Lily asked.

He nodded. "I'm quite proficient."

"Just keep in mind, you're needed," she said and mouthed the word *alive.*

"Understood." Tony left the cabin and found a position on the portside of the boat near the stern, staying low and out of sight of the other craft skimming across the water toward them, a machine gun mounted on a turret, aiming toward the Lost Cause. Tony prayed the boat didn't live up to its name that day.

The future of his small children, the captain and the passengers depended on the boat making it back to port safely.

Above him, he could hear Marcus on the radio calling out, "Mayday! Mayday! Mayday!"

As the boat approached, Tony held his fire, hoping the attackers weren't planning on actually shooting that wicked-looking machine gun.

As he looked out over the water, he could see that they were still several miles from shore. The Lost

Cause was a fast boat, but not nearly as fast as the attack boat gaining on them.

Holding on to the rail, he aimed his rifle the best he could, staring through the scope at the guy manning the machine gun. He held on with difficulty as the little boat bounced across the waves, racing toward them. If he did fire, the likelihood of hitting them would be slim, unless they slowed to give their shooter a more stable base to fire from.

Even Tony couldn't get a good bead on the gunman with the Lost Cause powering through the ocean's waves.

Just when he thought their attackers might not use the machine gun, the gunman opened fire.

Bullets flew overhead, some hit the boat, but most missed.

Tony worried about Marcus exposed above at the helm. If he'd been hit, he wasn't letting it stop him. He aimed the boat at the shore, giving it all the power he could.

Tony braced himself as best he could, aimed at the man behind the machine gun, waited for the second he appeared in his scope's crosshairs and pulled the trigger.

The gunman's arm jerked back, and he stopped firing.

Another man yanked him aside and took control of the automatic weapon.

Tony aimed again, knowing it had been mostly

luck that his bullet had found his target. The chances of hitting the second gunman were pretty slim. Despite the odds, he braced, aimed and waited for the man to bounce into his crosshairs. When he did, he noticed the gunman was aiming directly at him.

Tony squeezed the trigger.

The bullet must have hit the machine gun, knocking it sideways as the gunman pulled the trigger. The bullets hit the water several yards to the right of the Lost Cause.

By the time the gunman straightened the weapon, Marcus had pulled ahead, putting a little more distance between them. The bullets from the machine gun fell short of the stern. But that wouldn't be for long.

Suddenly, two speedboats ripped past the Lost Cause, heading straight for the attack boat.

Tony sat up and watched as the men on the speed boats brought out what appeared to be assault rifles and turned them on the attackers.

The machine gunman redirected his aim at one of the speed boats only to be fired on by men from the other boats. Apparently realizing they were outnumbered, the attack boat driver spun the boat around and raced off in the opposite direction.

The speed boats went after them for several miles, ultimately turning around to follow the Lost Cause into shore.

Marcus pulled the boat alongside the dock, shut

down the engine and dropped down from the helm to the deck. "Are you okay?" he asked Tony.

Tony nodded and hurried to open the door to the cabin. "Lily, Robbie, Mari?"

"We're all okay," Lily said, holding Robbie against her.

Mari blinked and opened her eyes. "I'm hungry."

Tony laughed, the adrenaline rush he'd been riding all the way back to shore, starting to fade. He helped Lily to her feet, lifted Robbie into his arms and waited while Lily picked up Mari. They stepped out of the boat onto the dock and waited for the occupants of the speed boats to disembark.

Tony wanted to know who these people were who'd come to their rescue.

Three men climbed out of the speedboats and joined them on the dock. The first one approached Tony. "Are you Antonio Delossantos?"

Tony stepped forward and held out his hand. "I am."

The tall, muscular man held out his hand. "Hank Patterson. I'm the founder of the Brotherhood Protectors."

Tony shot a glance toward Marcus. "The outfit Marcus sent for?"

Hank nodded. "We came as soon as I could muster enough men to make a difference. We arrived a couple hours ago."

"How did you know we would need help or where to find us?" Tony asked.

Marcus held up what appeared to be a metal button. "I gave them my GPS tracking device number before they left Montana. I thought they might want to know where we were since they'd be arriving while we were out to sea."

"Damned lucky you did." Tony clapped a hand against Marcus's shoulder. "Thank you. And thank you for some fancy boating skills."

Marcus puffed out his chest. "Learned everything I know from my days assigned to SEAL Boat Team 22 out of Stennis, Mississippi. The boats weren't the same, but the techniques were similar."

Hank shook hands with Marcus, a grin stretching across his face. "Long time no see, man. I thought you were dead."

"Not dead, just hidden away in my own little piece of paradise." He pulled Hank into a hug. "Thanks for coming out to meet our welcoming party."

"Again, how did you know we'd be in trouble?" Tony asked.

Hank's smile faded. "When we got to the hotel, the staff was in a panic and all gathered around whatever television they could find."

"Why?" Tony asked, a sinking feeling hitting him in the gut. His arm tightened around Robbie.

"Some guy escaped from prison in San José."

Hank stared straight into Tony's eyes. "A drug cartel kingpin by the name of El Patron."

Tony felt as if he'd been sucker punched in the belly. "When?"

Hank's lips pressed into a thin line. "Early this morning."

The nightmare Tony thought he'd put to bed when he'd helped capture El Patron had come back to haunt him.

Bile rose up Lily's throat. She swallowed hard to keep from losing her lunch in front of the children. Now was not the time to be weak. Tony needed her to stay strong. Robbie and Mari needed her to protect them from whatever horrors El Patron might have in mind as revenge against Tony for putting him in jail for the past two years.

Lily hugged Mari close. She couldn't let anything happen to the children. They were innocent and deserved a chance at a long and happy life.

One by one, Hank Patterson introduced this team of former special operations soldiers, sailors and marines, using only their callsigns.

"This is Swede, Navy SEAL," he said of the tallest man with the light blond hair.

Tony shook hands with the SEAL and thanked him for helping them out of a tight situation.

Hank pointed to a broad-shouldered man with brown hair. "That's Duke from Delta Force."

"Taz was an Army Ranger. Chuck and Boomer, Navy SEALs."

Tony shook hands with all of them and thanked them for coming on such short notice.

"Let's get back to the hotel," Marcus said. "I don't like that you're out in the open."

Tony helped Lily load the children into the back of one of the SUVs there to take them back. Marcus climbed in with Hank as his team filled two other SUVs.

Robbie sat silently beside Tony, his hand inside his father's, his brow wrinkled.

Lily could only imagine what was going on in the child's mind.

He had to know the people on the other boat had been shooting at them. With the sound of gunfire from the other boat as well as from the boat they were on, it would've been hard to keep that knowledge from him. Robbie was a smart little boy. Too bad he had to be exposed to the violence of a drug cartel at such a young age. He hadn't been old enough to remember much about his mother's death. Only that she hadn't come home one day, and then there was a funeral. He was old enough now to have nightmares about this day.

As they entered the hotel, they found the staff clustered in groups, whispering quietly, their brows furrowed, worry apparent in their voices and expressions.

Tony handed Mari to Lily. "Please, take them up to our room."

Lily wanted to protest but knew he was right. Robbie saw too much.

As she took Robbie's hand in hers, she heard Tony saying, "We need to send our guests home." He started toward the registration desk.

Marcus stopped him with a hand on his arm. "Look, we don't know if El Patron will come here. He might want to stay out of jail rather than risk you putting him back behind bars."

Tony snorted. "El Patron will come for me. Of that, I'm certain." He pinched the bridge of his nose. "How soon is the only question. And he won't stop at hurting me. The man will be out for revenge." He met Marcus's gaze and lowered his voice so that Robbie couldn't overhear him. Tony clenched his fists. "We need to get my family on the next plane out of San Jose."

Lily's breath caught in her throat. Leave Costa Rica? She didn't want to go. Not if Tony wasn't with them. Again, she knew she didn't have a choice. She had to do what was best for the children. If taking them back to Texas was the answer, so be it. She hurried Robbie and Mari toward the elevator and whisked them up to the room where she had them bathe and dress for dinner. Then she left the television on, playing a cartoon movie while she ducked into the bathroom, showered quickly and dressed in a long white dress that fit her body to perfection. With the door open to the bedroom, she dried her hair, applied a mascara to her eyelashes and dabbed on a soft pink lipstick. Satisfied with how she looked, she moved the children to the living room and read books with them, waiting for their father to arrive and take them to dinner.

Robbie sat next to her, pressed up against her side. Quieter than she'd ever known him. After she'd finished one short book, he looked up at her and asked, "Why did the men on the other boot shoot at us?"

Lily's heart squeezed hard in her chest. She wished Tony was there to answer his son's questions. She couldn't be sure of what he'd want her to say. All she could do was be truthful. "They were bad people."

"Will they try to kill my papi?" he asked.

"Oh, Robbie," she hugged him to her. "Your father is a smart man. He will be okay."

"I love Papi," Mari said.

Lily's eyes filled with tears. "That's right, Mari. You love your Papi."

"I love him, too," Robbie said, his voice higher than usual due to strain. "I don't want him to go away like my mama did."

"He's not leaving you or Mari," Lily said. She

prayed she was right. Robbie and Mari needed their father. He was all they had.

"El Patron killed my wife. He's not above murdering children," Tony said to Marcus. "We have to get Robbie, Mari and Lily on the next plane back to the States."

Hank arrived with his team in the lobby in time to catch Tony's last words. "I hate to be the bearer of more bad news, but have you looked at the weather lately? If you try to fly your family out now, your kids will be no safer on an airplane headed for the States than staying here. You know that hurricane that was off the coast of the Baja peninsula? Well, it's moving inland and is creating a massive low-pressure system they expect to stretch across all of Mexico and up into Texas. We dodged it on our way down. By now, it'll be wreaking havoc with the airways. Airports in Houston and Dallas were expected to shut down by tonight."

Tony shook his head. "Hank, you don't understand. El Patron will come after my children to get to me."

Hank shook his head. "There's no way you'll get them out tonight. It takes three hours to get to the airport. By the time you arrive, the flights to the US will be cancelled until that storm moves on."

Tony slammed his fist into his palm. "It's not safe

here. And my being at the hotel puts everyone here at risk."

"That's why we're here," Hank said. "We'll provide perimeter security and keep you and your guests secure."

Tony raked a hand through his hair, wanting to argue, but he knew Hank was right. "Thanks."

"I'll fill in on either the day or night shift," Marcus said. "I cancelled my boat tours for tomorrow. However, I need to go over the boat and make sure none of the bullet holes will sink it before I take it out again."

"Whatever it takes to fix it, send me the bill," Tony said. "And again, thank you. I don't know what I'd do without you."

"Hey, you helped me when I was at the lowest point in my life. The least I can do is help you and those kids." Marcus clapped a hand against his shoulder. "That's what friends do."

CHAPTER 9

Lily must have fallen asleep. She jerked awake when the door to the room opened and Tony walked in.

His face was grim, and his eyes hollow. He appeared as if he'd aged ten years in the past few hours.

Lily untangled herself from Robbie and Mari. Both had fallen asleep while she'd read to them, tired from their eventful day fishing, snorkeling, and then dodging bullets.

When she straightened, she went to Tony, wrapping her arms around his waist. "It's going to be all right," she whispered.

"How can it be?" he said. "You're in danger. Robbie and Mari are in danger. I've brought you all into this, and now I might lose you." He buried his face in her hair and held her close.

Lily stood steady, giving him as much strength as she could. The man had lost so much and feared losing the rest of what meant the most to him. His children.

Tony raised his head, captured her cheeks between his palms and turned her face up to his. "I'm sorry I brought you into this."

She shook her head. "I'm not. I'm glad I'm here to help you keep Robbie and Mari safe."

He stared down into her eyes. "I don't know what I did to deserve you."

She smiled. "You had the good sense to hire me as your au pair."

"You're fired," he said.

"What?" Lily frowned. "Why?"

"I have a rule I can't break. I don't get involved with my employees." He lowered his mouth to within a hair's breadth of hers. "If you work for me, I can't kiss you."

"Oh." She rested her hands on his chest. "And you want to…kiss me?"

"More than I want to take my next breath. You're fired," he repeated.

"Good. Because I don't get involved with my clients, and I want so very much to kiss you. And now that I no longer work for you…" She leaned up on her toes and pressed her mouth to his.

As if he'd been released from restraints, Tony crushed her to him, his lips moving over hers like a starving man searching for sustenance.

Lily opened to him, thrusting her tongue out to meet his in a long, sensuous caress. She pressed her body to his, wanting to be closer, frustrated by the clothing keeping their skin from touching.

When Tony pushed back, Lily dragged in deep, steadying breaths.

"I reek of fish, and you smell like a rose garden." He leaned his forehead against hers. "Let me shower and change, and we can go down to dinner."

"Okay," Lily said, her head still spinning from the incredible kiss that had completely rocked her world. She didn't want him to leave her standing there. Not when there were more kisses to be had. Then she remembered the children were in the same room with them.

She spun, expecting to see them staring wide-eyed up at her, demanding to know what she was doing with their father.

Lily let out a relieved sigh when she realized they were still sound asleep. She hadn't been sure how she would have explained why their au pair was no longer their au pair, and why she'd been kissing their father. The kiss was such a new development, even Lily wasn't sure what to think of it.

Had he kissed her because she was there and could give comfort? Would he regret it later when he wasn't so distressed?

Lily would never regret it. Even if it was the only

kiss she ever received from him. Deep down, she'd wanted it to happen, even when she hadn't known she'd wanted it. The man turned her inside out, exposing emotions she'd never felt for another man. Could he be the one she'd waited her entire life to find?

And if he was her one and only, would he consider her for a second chance at finding love?

Lily didn't know how to compete with his first wife. The woman was dead and enshrined as a saint in Tony's mind. How could any woman measure up to that?

Slow down, girl. Lily had to coach herself to breathe. Tony had only kissed her. He hadn't mentioned anything beyond that. Lily's mind had shot ahead as if they were destined to end up in love, married and raising Robbie and Mari, together, as a family.

You got far too much sun, she told herself. It must have fried her brain and made her see things that weren't there. He'd only kissed her, nothing more.

Lily left the living area and hurried to the other bathroom where she pressed a cool cloth to her heated cheeks. Perhaps she was running a fever. That would explain why she was hallucinating and dreaming of things that couldn't possibly happen between a rich hotelier and a kindergarten teacher from a small town in Texas.

She touched her fingers to her swollen lips, still

feeling the electric tingles he'd inspired that had shot throughout her body and low in her belly.

Lily moaned softly and pressed a hand to her flat stomach. She wanted so much more than just a kiss.

"Auntie Lily?" Robbie called out.

Lily dropped the cloth on the counter and hurried out to the living room where Robbie was waking up. Mari yawned and rubbed her fists against her eyes. "I'm hungry," she said as she opened her eyes.

"I'm hungry, too," Tony said from the doorway to his bedroom

He'd showered, shaved and dressed in dark trousers and a crisp white shirt. His hair was combed neatly back on his head, and he looked so handsome Lily thought she might cry.

Never had she been so taken with a man as she was with Tony.

He held out his hand for Robbie and another for Lily.

Lily laid her hand in his palm, and he curled his fingers around hers.

Mari slid off the sofa and reached for Lily's other hand.

They left the room as a united front and descended to the restaurant.

Robbie was quiet throughout the meal, but Mari, who'd missed the action and danger of gunfire, chattered on in a mix of Spanish and English about the big fish she'd caught. "Do we get to eat the big fish?" she asked.

"Mr. Marcus is having the fish prepared. We can have some of it for dinner tomorrow night," Tony said.

Mari clapped her hands and bounced in her booster seat. "I want snapper," she sang.

Lily smiled. "I think your daughter likes fishing."

"What did you like best, Robbie," Tony asked. "Fishing or snorkeling?"

Robbie's eyes grew round and filled with tears. "I hate both. And I hate riding in boats." He pushed back from the table and ran out of the restaurant.

"I'll go to him." Lily rose.

Tony put a hand on her arm, already out of his own chair. "No, I'll talk to him."

"He's afraid," Lily said. "Of losing you."

Mari's eyes pooled with tears. "Robbie's sad. I'm sad, too." She burst into tears.

"Go on. We'll be up in the room." Lily lifted Mari and hugged her in her arms. "Come on, *mi amor*. Let's go to bed."

"I don't want to go…to…bed," she cried, between sobs. "I want Robbie."

"He'll be up in a minute. Let's go brush our teeth, and we can read a book while we wait for him."

Mari rubbed her eyes and sniffled. "Can we read the book about the lost lamb?"

"Yes, of course." Lily carried Mari up to the room, changed her into her pajamas, washed her face and hands and had her brush her teeth. Still, Robbie and Tony hadn't come back to the room.

Settling Mari into her bed, Lily kicked off her heels, sat on the bed beside Mari and drew her feet up under her as she read to the little girl.

All the while, she worried about Robbie. Had he run out of the building? Were they gone so long because Tony couldn't find him? Twice, she almost got up and called down to the lobby to ask if Robbie had been found. And twice, she resisted. Tony would find his son. She had to believe that he would. She loved that little guy as if he were her own.

Lily faced the fact she was in deep with this family. If things didn't work out between her and Tony, she'd be in for a whole lot of heartache.

TONY CAUGHT up with Robbie in the hallway outside the restaurant. He took the boy's hand and walked him down the grand staircase and out into the courtyard where the pool was lit up like a shining blue rectangle in the darkness

Though there were guests still swimming, Tony led Robbie to a deserted end of the pool and sat with him on one of the lounge chairs. For a few minutes they sat in the darkness, side by side on the same lounge, their hands locked behind their heads, staring up at the night sky.

Robbie had stopped crying and lay silent, a stray hiccup the only sound coming from him.

Tony searched for words that could help his son get past his fear. But he couldn't get past his own. He tried several times to say something but couldn't. Finally, he said, "Miss Grayson is a good teacher, isn't she?"

Beside him, Robbie nodded.

"You know, she taught me something, too."

Robbie turned his head and looked at him. "She did?"

"Not the usual things like math, reading or writing, but something even more important."

Robbie turned on his side and propped himself up on his elbow. "What was that?"

"To notice the things and people around me." He slipped his arm around his son. "I was so sad about losing your mother, I didn't pay attention to what I still had. And what was that?" He smiled at Robbie.

"Me and Mari," Robbie said.

"That's right. She reminded me that I still had you two, and that I should love each and every moment I have with you."

"I miss mama," Robbie said.

Tony's heart pinched in his chest. "I miss her, too. But that doesn't mean I can't be happy and enjoy being with you and Mari. Your mama would have wanted us to fish, snorkel and spend time together. She would have loved seeing you catch your first fish. Just like Lily and I loved watching. It's okay to be happy."

"But those bad men…" Robbie's eyes teared up again.

"They can't take your happiness away without your permission. You get to keep your happiness. Just because they were bad doesn't mean you can't have good memories of your time with me, Mari and Lily. Those are your memories to keep forever."

Robbie nodded then swallowed hard. "Will they come back?"

"I don't know. But we will be brave no matter what." Tony touched a finger to Robbie's temple. "And we will have our memories tucked away in the backs of our minds, to bring out when we're scared or lonely, to cheer us up."

Robbie rolled to his back and tucked his hands behind his head again. For a long time, he lay there without saying a word.

Tony thought his son might have fallen asleep.

"Papi, I don't hate fishing," he said softly,

"I know you don't."

"And I don't hate snorkeling," he continued. "And I love you and Miss Grayson and will remember the good parts of today when I feel sad or lonely."

"That's my boy," Tony smiled up at the sky. "Remember the good times." He should have taken his own advice long ago, instead of wallowing in his grief and forgetting the goodness he'd had with Marisol and the good times yet to come with his children.

They lay in the lounge chair for a little longer without talking.

"Papi?"

"Yes, *hijo*?"

"Are you going to marry Miss Grayson?" Robbie asked.

The question caught Tony by surprise. "Why do you ask?"

"I saw you kissing her. Aren't you supposed to be married to kiss someone?"

Tony laughed. "A lot of people kiss without being married."

"Do you love Miss Grayson?" Robbie persisted.

Tony thought about it. He'd been absolutely certain of his love for Marisol from the moment he'd met her to the day she'd died.

Lily had been like a burr under his saddle from the moment he'd met her. She'd grown on him, slipping beneath his defenses until he couldn't get her out of his mind. And the kiss they'd shared…

Now, he'd never get her out of his mind. And he wasn't so sure he wanted to. He liked her drive, determination and spunkiness. And he loved how she was protective of the ones she loved, and how loyal she was to her family. If he was to fall in love, Lily would be a good choice. He wanted her. To kiss her, hold her and make love to her. But love her? Was it possible to fall in love a second time in one life?

"I don't know, Robbie," Tony said. "Maybe."

CHAPTER 10

EXHAUSTED from their day in the sun, Lily had changed into her flamingo pajamas and sat on the sofa waiting for Tony and Robbie to return to the room. After a while, she must have fallen asleep. The next thing she knew, she was being lifted in Tony's arms and carried to her bed.

She blinked up at him and slid her arms around his neck. "Did you and Robbie work things out?"

"Uh-huh," he said and brushed a kiss across her lips.

"I'm glad. He's had it rough."

"Yes, he has."

"Do I need to get him into his PJs and tuck him in?" She laid her cheek against his chest, loving the reassuring beat of his heart thumping against her ear.

"No. He's already in bed, sound asleep."

She looked up into his dark eyes. "No book?"

He shook his head. "Too tired." Then he placed her on her little bed in the living room.

Lily didn't want to let go of him. "Are you too tired?"

He chuckled. "Why? Are you going to read to me?"

"If you want me to," she said and leaned up and pressed her lips against his. "I'm all for reading, but I'd rather kiss."

"Kissing can be dangerous," he said touching his mouth to her forehead.

"Agreed. Apparently, we're danger magnets, today." Lily chuckled and pulled him down to her. "My bed's small, but I'm willing to share." She scooted to the side, making room for him.

He kissed a path down her neck to where her pulse beat fast at the base of her throat. "My bed's bigger, and not out in the middle of the living room."

"I was wondering if you'd figure that out."

He scooped her up in his arms and carried her into his bedroom, closing the door mostly, but not all the way. "You're still fired."

"If you hadn't fired me, I'd quit." She nuzzled the side of his neck and sighed. "How long is it socially acceptable for a girl to wait to sleep with a man she's just met?"

He laid her on the bed and raised a hand, counting off on his fingers. "How many days have we known each other?"

"Counting today?" Lily laughed. "A lifetime. When you were out there shooting at the attacking boat, time stood still for at least a century."

"I'd say that's long enough." Tony pulled his shirt out of his waistband and started unbuttoning it.

Lily rose up on her knees, pushed his hands aside and finished. Then she shoved the shirt over his broad shoulders and down his arms, admiring the way his muscles flexed when he moved. The shirt fell to the floor, and Lily reached for the button on his trousers.

He laid his hand over hers. "Once we start, there's no going back."

"I don't want to go back." Lily sighed. "And if there is no 'us' tomorrow, I'll be happy we had tonight." She looked up. "Hell, what I'm trying to say is that I'm not expecting anything out of tomorrow. No obligation. I won't cling and call you a hundred times to ask why you haven't called me. So, you're safe."

"What if I want to call you?"

Lily shrugged with a wicked smile. "I might answer the phone." She rested her hand on his chest, drew in a deep breath and let it out. "Are we doing this, or are we talking? You never know when one of the little people will wake with a nightmare."

He arched an eyebrow. "I'm game."

"So am I." She reached for the hem of her night shirt, and pulled it over her head, tossing it to the side, not too far out of reach. Having shed her bra earlier, she was naked from the waist up. "Your turn."

He unbuttoned his trousers and stepped out of them and his boxers.

Her gaze snagged on his erection. Then she smiled and wrapped her hands around his shaft. "I was beginning to wonder if I was even remotely turning you on."

"You have your answer." He backed away and held up a finger. "Hold that thought." Then he walked to the door and peeked out into the living room.

"Any sign of little people?" Lily asked as she slipped out of her flamingo pajama bottoms and panties.

Tony closed the door and turned to find her standing there in nothing but a smile.

His eyes flared as he crossed the room and took her into his arms. "I've wanted to do this all day."

"What was stopping you, besides children, employees and drug cartels?" She cocked an eyebrow and cupped his cheek in her palm. "Are you sure you're ready for this? No regrets. No guilt."

He nodded. "I'm ready."

"Good, because I can't wait another minute." Lily wrapped her arms around his neck and pressed her body against his.

Skin to skin felt even better than she'd dreamed. She slid her calf around the back of his leg and rubbed her center across the top of his thigh. The friction made her breath catch. Being naked wasn't enough. She wanted so much more.

Tony ran his hands down her back and over the swells of her buttocks, catching her at the backs of her thighs and lifting her off the ground.

Lily wrapped her legs around his waist, her entrance poised over his hard shaft. "Before we go there..."

"Protection?" He laid her on the bed and reached into the nightstand, pulled out an accordion of condoms and tossed them on the pillow beside her. "Will that be enough?"

"Maybe for tonight." She dragged her finger down her torso to the tuft of hair over her mons and slipped it in between her folds, touching herself where she wanted him to touch her. "I'm guessing it's been a while. Do you remember how to do this?"

He climbed over her, nudged her knees apart and settled his body between them. "I think I can remember. Making love is like riding a bike. You never forget how."

"Hmm. Not sure I like the analogy. Am I supposed to be the bike?"

"If the bike fits, ride it...?" He captured her lips in a deep, soul-defining kiss that stole any other words she might have said and left her breathless and eager for more. His cock pressed against her entrance but didn't push inward.

Lily lifted her knees and dug her heels into the

mattress, pushing up her hips, wanting him inside her.

Instead of pressing in, he touched her with his lips, tasting, nipping and traveling across every inch of her skin, working his way down to her breasts.

There, he took one crest in his mouth, then tongued, flicked and rolled the nipple until it tightened into a firm bead.

Lily moaned softly and writhed beneath him.

He shifted to the other breast and treated it to the same sweet torture. When he had her so wound up she thought she might explode, he moved down her torso with his tongue and mouth, blazing a path to the thatch of hair at the apex of her thighs. He parted her folds with his thumbs and dove in, taking the little strip of flesh into his mouth, flicking, sucking and laving it.

Lily hovered on the edge of orgasm, her body tense...waiting...waiting...

Then Tony flicked her clit one last time and sent her spiraling out of control. The electric shocks started at her core and rippled across her nerves to the very tips of her fingers and toes.

She rode the wave of sensations all the way to the end, collapsing against the mattress, breathing like a runner at the end of a marathon.

Lily paused for only a moment, her satisfaction nearly complete, but needing more to make it perfect. She dug her fingers into Tony's thick black hair and dragged him up her body. "I want you. Inside. Now." Reaching to the side, she grabbed the string of condoms, ripped one free and tore it open. Her hands shook with her need.

Tony took the condom from her and rolled it down over his shaft. He pressed the tip to her entrance and bent to take her mouth, thrusting his tongue past her teeth as he drove himself home inside her.

Her hands on his buttocks, Lily guided him in and out, setting a slow pace at first, increasing the speed with her level of need.

He took over, rocking in and out of her, hard and deep.

She dug her heels into the mattress and raised her hips, meeting him thrust for thrust.

Tony's body grew rigid. He drove deep one last time and held himself there, his cock pulsing with the force of his release. Then he dropped down on her, rolling her to the side and into his embrace.

She lay there, her cheek resting against his naked chest. "Wow."

"Agreed," he murmured against her temple.

"I wish we could stay like this forever," she said, snuggling closer.

"Me, too."

Lily sighed. "Alas, we can't."

"No, we can't." Tony chuckled. "It was hard enough to explain to Robbie why we were kissing."

"He saw that?" Lily shook her head. "Not much gets past that kid." She leaned up and kissed him one last time, and then rolled out of the bed and onto her feet. It took her a few moments to locate her pajamas and her panties. Once she was wearing them, she turned back to Tony.

He'd risen and slipped into a pair of boxer shorts. He pulled her into his arms and rested his chin on the top of her head. "Can I call you?"

She laughed. "If you want. I might answer." Then she quietly slipped out of his room, relieved to find the living room empty of children. She checked on Robbie and Mari, tucking their blankets under their chins and bending to kiss them, again.

When she looked up, she caught Tony watching from the doorframe.

"You really are good to them," he whispered.

"It helps if you like them," she said and moved to pass him.

He put out his arm and blocked her exit. "It does help if you like them. And I love them more than I ever imagined."

Lily's heart swelled. She loved them, too. And she was well on her way to falling in love with their father.

CHAPTER 11

Tony woke the next morning to the incessant ringing of the phone on his nightstand. He rolled over to look at the green glow of the digital clock. Five o'clock in the morning. Who in the hell would call him that early on the house phone?

He lifted the receiver. "Yeah."

"Tony, it's Hank. We've been monitoring the weather and flight status. There's a break in the storms, and the airlines are flying out of San José to Texas. If you want to get your kids on one of those flights, now would be the time. I know it takes three hours to drive them to the airport. If they get on the road now, they can get to the airport in time to catch the noon flight out."

"On it. Thanks for the heads-up." Tony flung the covers aside and rolled out of bed and onto his feet.

"Everything all right?" Lily poked her head

through the door, her hair mussed, and her face flushed from sleep. “I heard the phone ring.”

“The airlines are flying out of San José today. They’ve had a break in the weather. We need to gather the children and get on the road as soon as possible.”

Her eyes widened. “You’re sending them back to the States?”

“Yes. I’m sending you, Robbie and Mari back to Texas until we figure out what to do about El Patron.” He didn’t want to, not after what had happened between him and Lily the night before. Everything seemed so new and fragile.

Lily frowned. “You aren’t coming with us.”

“Just because I leave doesn’t mean El Patron will give up on his plot for revenge. He’ll go after my holdings, my staff and my friends. I can’t leave them to deal with the backlash.”

Lily went to Tony and wrapped her arms around his waist. “I wish I could stay and help.”

He pressed a kiss against her temple. “You’ll be helping me more by making sure my children make it safely back to Texas and are well and happy there until I return.”

She nodded and looked up into his eyes. “Will you call me?”

He winked. “I might.”

She leaned up on her toes and kissed his lips. “I might answer.”

Tony pulled her into a tight hug, not wanting to let go but not wanting her to remain in the path of El Patron's wrath. He sighed and set her at arm's length. "Getting you and the kids back to the States is the right thing to do."

"I agree. We can't let that monster hurt Robbie and Mari. I'll do my best to make sure they arrive safely, and I'll stick around until you return."

He kissed her forehead. "Thank you."

She squared her shoulders and lifted her chin. "We'd better get moving if we want to get to the airport in time for the flight out."

"I'd send you via private jet, but I'm not sure I can arrange one fast enough to take advantage of the break in the weather."

"We'll survive on a commercial flight." She laughed. "I don't want to get spoiled flying charter. Although, it was really nice."

"I'll see what I can arrange," he promised.

"I'll get the kids up, dressed and packed while you make the flight arrangements, whatever they are." Lily hurried into the other bedroom and kissed Robbie and Mari awake.

THE CHILDREN WEREN'T TOO happy about getting up before the sun. Lily had to dress them while they sat up half-asleep. Then she packed a suitcase each containing a couple changes of clothing and their favorite toys. Their father could ship the rest of their things to them later.

"Why do we have to leave?" Robbie asked. "Is it because of the bad guys?"

"Bad guys," Mari repeated while hugging her doll and rocking back and forth.

"Your father thinks it would be better if we go back home to Texas until they catch the bad guys and put them in jail."

Robbie brightened. "Then can we come back and go fishing again?"

Lily bit her lip to keep from asking him when he'd stopped hating fishing. Apparently, whatever talk he'd had with Tony had made him feel better about their day on the boat before they'd been attacked. "I'm not sure if we'll be back this summer. But I'm staying with you at the ranch until your father comes home."

"Yay!" Robbie cried and flung his arms around her. "I love you, mama."

Mari ran over to Lily and flung her arms around her legs. "I love you, mama."

A lump formed in Lily's throat. She didn't have the heart to remind them that she wasn't their mother. Robbie had blurted it out without realizing what he was saying. Mari had mimicked her brother.

Both statements had gone straight to Lily's heart. She would love being Robbie and Mari's mother. They were such good kids, and they deserved to be loved and happy. Swallowing hard, she refused to shed tears. They had too much to do to get on the road in time to make the flight through the break in the weather.

When they were dressed and packed, Lily met Tony in the living room.

He'd been on the phone since she'd left him, but he'd managed to pull on his clothes and shoes while making arrangements to fly his family to Texas.

"Good news," he said. "I arranged for a charter flight that will leave out a few minutes earlier than the commercial flight. They're pretty sure you'll make it over or between the storm clouds in time. If they think the situation will be too dangerous, they'll divert to someplace else safer to land and wait out the storm."

"We packed sufficient clothing to hole up somewhere for a few days, if we have to," Lily said. "And toys for entertainment."

Robbie reached for his father's hand. "Can't you come with us, Papi?"

Tony squatted down beside his son. "You know I would if I could." He hugged Robbie and then Mari. "I love you both so much. Robbie, I'm counting on you to take good care of your sister." To Mari he said, "And Mari, I want you to listen to Miss Grayson. She's going to help Robbie take care of you."

"*Te amo,* Papi." Her bottom lip quivered, and she flung her arms around her father's neck.

"Are you coming with us to the airport?" Lily asked.

"Yes and no," he said evasively. "I'm setting up a bait and switch deal. The short answer is no. I won't be with you on the trip to San José. But yes, I'll be at the airport to see you off."

Lily swallowed her disappointment and tried to be brave. "I understand."

"If anyone is following us, I want them to come after me, not you and the kids."

"Then this is the last time we'll have together, just you and us," Lily said. She looked up into his face. "Remember, I quit."

He grinned. "No, I fired you."

"Whatever." She reached out and grabbed the front of his shirt, bringing him close. "Kiss me like you mean it," she demanded.

"Oh, darlin', I mean it all right." And he proceeded to prove it, kissing her until she almost passed out from lack of oxygen.

"*Te amo,* Tony," she whispered ever so softly she was sure he wouldn't hear.

He leaned back and brushed a strand of her hair back behind her ear. "Lily, you've changed my life."

She chuckled. "I hope in a good way."

He brushed her lips with his. "In a very good way. I'm not letting go of that." Tony reached into his pocket and pulled out a chain with a pretty amber stone pendant. "I want you to wear this until I see you again. It's not anything special, just something that will remind you of me." He looped it over her head.

Lily tucked it under her shirt, close to her heart. He could have given her an old rock, and she'd have felt as treasured.

Tony squatted beside Mari and pulled a similar but shorter chain from his pocket with a pink stone and looped it over Mari's head. "A pretty for my pretty *hija*."

Mari grinned and flung her arms around her father's neck. "*Te amo,* Papi."

"What about me?" Robbie said.

Tony straightened. "I figured a necklace wouldn't do for my little man. He pulled a shiny silver disk-like coin from his pocket and handed it to Robbie. "This is a lucky coin. Keep it in your pocket, and you will have good luck on the trip back to Texas."

Robbie stared down at the disk and smiled. "*Gracias,* Papi." He put it in his pocket and hugged his father. "I will keep it always."

Then they were on their way down the elevator and climbing into one of the two SUVs that would be making the trip to San José. Tony explained that the second SUV would contain Hank and two of his guys.

Marcus and Tony would ride with Lily and the kids to start with. Then they would stop for fuel along the way and switch it up, car and all.

"They want me," he said, his gaze steady. "I'm going to divert El Patron's men away from you and the kids. If they attack anything, it will be the vehicle I'm in."

Lily would rather have kept the family together, but she understood what they were attempting. At this point, keeping the children safe was more important than keeping them with their father.

They started off in the two SUVs, moving northwest on Highway 34. In the little village of Parrita, they stopped at a service station.

Mari and Robbie both had to use the bathroom. Lily accompanied them to the restroom inside the station while Tony, Marcus, Hank and Hank's men covered the building, both inside and out.

Lily was finishing up, washing Mari and Robbie's hands when an explosion rocked the building. Plaster and dust shook free from the ceiling, showering down on them and making the bathroom cloudy with a fine haze of powdery dust.

Lily shielded Robbie and Mari with her body, shock making her freeze where she stood. When the shaking stopped, Lily pulled herself together and tried the door. It was jammed. Bracing her foot on the wall, she pulled with all her might. She had to get the children out of the building quickly, before the roof and walls caved in on top of them.

On her third attempt to open the door, it finally budged enough for her to get her arm and shoulder through the space. Leaning her back into it, she got the door open enough to get out and bring the children with her.

The station was in shambles, the path to the front impossible to navigate with the ceiling hanging down and live wires exposed.

Lily turned toward the back exit. The explosion had blown the door open, and sunlight shone in, reflecting off the dust particles and creating a bright haze she couldn't quite see through.

Grasping Robbie and Mari's hands in hers, she ran for the back of the building and burst out into the open.

Hands grabbed her. She released her hold on the children and went into defense mode, jerking her knee upward, hitting the man in the groin. Then she slammed the heel of her palm against his nose, driving the cartilage up into his head. He released her and grabbed his face.

But it was too late. Two other men had snatched the children and held them with hands over their mouths and guns pointed at their heads.

The dark-haired man with beady dark eyes holding Robbie growled low in a Hispanic accent, "Come quiet, or we will kill them."

Lily held up her hands in surrender. She couldn't do anything but meet their demands. Robbie and Mari's lives were at stake.

The man, whose nose she'd busted, pulled a gun and held it to her head,

"No," the other man said, softly. "No noise." He jerked his head toward a back alley and turned. Then he lifted Robbie in his arms and carried him away,

Mari kicked and bit the hand over her mouth. The man holding her clamped his hand over her mouth and nose.

"You'll suffocate her," Lilly cried out. "Let me take her. We won't fight." She couldn't escape, not when they had Robbie, and they had guns pointed and could kill any one of them with the twitch of a trigger finger.

Lily and the children were hurried down the back alley to a van and shoved inside.

Once she regained her balance, Lily pulled Robbie and Mari into her arms and held them tight. The men who'd captured her got in with them, and the driver pulled out of the alley and onto a side road, away from the main street.

How long would it take Tony, Hank and the others to figure out they were missing?

With the children huddled close, shivering from fear and crying softly, Lily prayed it wouldn't be long.

CHAPTER 12

When the explosion went off, Tony was thrown halfway across the inside of the station and hit his head against a brick wall. The force of the explosion must have knocked him out. How long he laid there in the rubble, he wasn't sure. When he came to, he pushed to his knees and looked around, blinking at the dust filling the air.

"Tony! Lily!" Marcus's voice sounded through the haze.

Something thick and warm dripped into Tony's eye, and he wiped it away. "Here," he said, his voice coming out as a croak. He coughed and tried again. "I'm here."

Marcus appeared through the fog of dust. "Tony, you all right?" He grabbed Tony's arm and helped him to his feet. "Where are the kids? Where's Lily?"

"Kids?" Tony shook his head, and the room spun. Then everything rushed back at him. "Lily. Robbie. Mari."

"That's right. Where are they?"

"They were in the bathroom. I was standing by the door." He looked around, his pulse pounding hard, pain throbbing in his head. "They were in the bathroom." He shoved Marcus's hand away from his arm and staggered through the debris toward the bathroom door.

Ceiling plaster and rubble lay against the half-open door.

Tony used his shoulder to shove the door wide open. The room was empty. He spun, his heart hammering, his vision blurring. "Where are they? We have to find them."

"There's a back door," Marcus said through the swirling dust.

Tony followed the silhouette of his friend through the cloud, out into the open air.

Hank and his men rounded the sides of the building, their faces and arms covered in cuts and scrapes.

"Someone shot a rocket at us," Hank called out. "Is everyone all right?"

"Tony's got a head injury," Marcus said. "My ears are ringing, but we're alive."

Tony turned to Hank. "Where are Lily and the kids? Tell me you have them."

Hank shook his head. "They were inside with you. When the rocket hit, we were all thrown."

"They must have been watching," Tony said. He pressed a hand to his forehead that had started stinging and felt a warm sticky liquid. When he pulled his hand away, it was covered in blood. He didn't care.

El Patron had his family.

"We have to find them," Tony said through gritted teeth. "We can't let Patron hurt them."

"Did you give them the tracking devices?" Hank asked.

Tony nodded, his head coming up, hope daring to fill his chest. "The tracking monitor. Where is it?"

"In the SUV." Hank turned and ran around the side of the building.

Tony and the rest of them followed.

The SUVs had taken a beating. One had suffered severe damage: the windows were shattered and two of the tires were flat. The other had been parked next to the solid side of the station where concrete bricks had shielded it from complete destruction.

Hank reached into the glove compartment of the rear vehicle, retrieved the hand-held device and turned it on.

Tony leaned over his shoulder, a hard knot lodged in his throat. El Patron had his family.

Madre de Dios, that bastard had his family.

It was all he could do not to fall to his knees in despair. Tony shook his head, the pain that shot through him reminding him that as long as he was alive, he'd find them, and he'd kill El Patron.

"There." Hank pointed at three bright green dots almost blended together on the screen. "They're traveling up…Highway 239, into the hills." He looked up. "Let's go."

With one of the vehicles out of commission, they transferred their weapons to the functioning SUV and all six of them climbed in.

Marcus took the driver's seat and Hank called shotgun. Tony sat behind Marcus and leaned through the middle to see the tracking device.

They sped out of Parrita and turned right at the junction of the two highways. The road was narrow and wound through the hills. They couldn't go too fast or they risked careening out of control and over the edge of the road.

Tony clenched his fists and prayed they caught up with El Patron's vehicle. And he prayed the cartel wouldn't kill Lily and the kids out of pure spite. If they wanted him badly enough, they'd use them as hostages for trade. Tony was all right with that. He'd rather die than any of them. And once he was dead, Patron would have his revenge. He wouldn't need to kill Tony's children and their au pair.

Deep down, Tony knew the chances of any of

them coming out alive were slim. If El Patron held the cards, he'd kill them all and be done with the Delossantos.

Tony glanced around at the dusty, dirty, scraped and scratched men who'd just survived a bombing. If anyone could help him get his family back, these were the men to do it.

He focused on the road ahead and the success of the mission. Believing was halfway to winning.

After at least an hour on the road, the van left the highway and bumped along a rutted path through dense vegetation. After being thrown around for twenty minutes more, they came to a halt and her captors got out of the van.

As the side door slid open, a shout rang out, "El Patron!"

Lily had known in the back of her mind that one of the men with her had to have been the infamous cartel kingpin. She had hoped she could affect an escape for the three of them before she ran into that particular man. He had a reputation for his cruelty, and Lily didn't want her or the children to be made the examples of his horrifying appetite for gore.

The driver and another man grabbed her arm and yanked her out of the van.

Lily kept her hold on Mari, refusing to let them

take her from her. Robbie cowered behind her, holding onto the hem of her shirt.

Already, Lily was sizing up her options, counting the number of her opponents and searching for potential escape routes.

The cartel camp was located well off the beaten path, deep in a tropical jungle with rugged hills rising above them.

If she could sneak the children past the men guarding her, she could hide in the jungle and make her way back to the main highway.

If she knew which way that was. Escaping through a jungle wasn't what would make it difficult. Running with two small children would be next to impossible. But to stay captive and risk El Patron killing them wasn't an option.

Lily and the children were taken to a small shack, smaller than the size of her dorm room in college. Hastily constructed of plywood and tin, it was situated at the back of the camp. They were shoved inside, and the door closed behind them. The sound of a bar sliding in place might as well have been a lock with no key. Mari clung to her, and Robbie leaned against her side, his fingers curling into her shirt.

With no windows, the room was dark. The only light was that which found its way around the cracks between the door and the frame and between the tin roof and the tops of the walls. Slowly, her vision adjusted to the darkness, and she took stock of her surroundings. The room was completely empty with nothing she could use as a weapon. The dirt floor was hardpacked. Digging their way out would be difficult with their bare hands.

"Are the bad men going to kill us?" Robbie asked, his voice catching on a sob.

"Not if I can help it," Lily said. "What I need you to do now is be strong for Mari. If we have a chance to get out of here, you need to be ready to run. Got it?"

Robbie nodded against her.

"Okay, let's see if there's a way to get out of here," she murmured.

The ceiling of the shack was nothing more than corrugated tin, sagging a little in the middle because whoever had built the shack hadn't bothered to use rafters. The only thing holding up the roof were the four walls.

Lily set Mari on her feet while she inspected the walls, pushing against the plywood, hoping to find a weak spot she could take advantage of. Having been constructed recently, the plywood was in reasonably good shape. It wasn't going to mold and fall apart anytime soon.

Looking up at the roof, she jumped and pressed her fingers to the corrugated tin. It moved, lifting up on one end near the wall. Her heart fluttered.

Could it be they hadn't nailed it to the wall at that point?

She jumped again, her fingers pushing against the tin, lifting it up. If she could push it high enough, they might be able to crawl over the edge and drop to the ground.

She dropped to her knees. "Robbie, get on my shoulders."

"Why?" he asked, while slinging his leg over her shoulder and straddling the back of her neck.

"I want you to push up on the ceiling to see how high it will go."

Robbie raised his hands above his head and pushed against the tin.

It rose, creating a gap big enough to fit a small adult through the opening.

Her heart beat hard in her chest. This could be their way out. All she had to do was figure out how to scale the wall without a ladder or stool to step up on.

A scraping sound indicated someone was pushing the bar across the door.

Lily lowered Robbie off her shoulders and set him on the ground. Then she took Robbie and Mari's hands and faced the door and the man who entered.

With his back to the sunlight, Lily couldn't make out his face. But by his commanding presence, she knew it was El Patron.

He shoved what appeared to be a satellite phone toward her. "You will call your boyfriend and tell him to be here within the hour, or I will start killing his children."

Robbie gasped beside her; his arm encircled her leg. He looked up at Lily, his eyes swimming in tears, "I don't want to die," Robbie whispered.

"You aren't going to," Lily said, raising her chin. She took the sat phone from El Patron and pressed the number she'd memorized for Tony's cellphone.

After the fourth ring, Tony answered, "Delossantos speaking."

His voice filled all the empty spaces in Lily's heart. "Tony?" She swallowed hard to keep a sob from rising up her throat.

"Are you okay? And the kids?"

"We're okay for now," she said.

"What do they want? I'll give them anything. Money, my hotel, anything."

El Patron jerked the sat phone from Lily's hand and spoke into it, "I want you, for them."

"As long as you don't hurt them, you've got a deal," Tony said, his voice sounding loud inside the hut. "Where do you want to make the trade?"

"I will notify you when and where." El Patron ended the call and sneered at Lily. "Let him wait. He can think about the years I spent rotting in prison." The man touched a finger to Lily's cheek. "Maybe I'll take what I want first. It's been a long two years."

Lily met his gaze, her eyes narrowing. If the man

tried to rape her, he'd soon find that he'd met his match. She lifted her chin, refusing to back down.

"*Muy bonita,*" he murmured and bent to press his lips to hers.

Shocked, Lily backed away.

Robbie darted forward. "Leave my Lily alone!" he yelled and kicked the man in the shin.

El Patron muttered a curse in Spanish and backhanded Robbie, sending him flying across the room.

Lily started forward, ready to take the man down for hurting Robbie. Before she could, Mari screamed and lunged toward El Patron.

Lily caught her and swung her up into her arms, holding her as she fought to get to the bastard who'd hit her brother.

El Patron laughed and left the building, slamming the door shut behind him.

Lily hurried to Robbie and helped him to his feet. Even in the shadows, she could see he had a split lip and a mark on his cheek that would soon become black and blue.

"He's a bad man," Robbie said, his bottom lip quivering.

Mari squirmed out of Lily's hold and wrapped her arms around her brother's neck, her body racked with sobs.

Lily had to get them out of there, before Patron returned to do even worse things to them.

She hated to ask Robbie, but she had no way of

pulling herself up to the edge of the wall. Her upper body strength wasn't enough to get her up that far. If she were just a couple feet taller, she might be able to pull herself up. "Robbie, do you think you could hold me up if I climb on your back?"

"I think so," he said

"Get on your hands and knees," she said and pointed to the ground, below the loose tin.

Robbie did as she asked.

"Tell me if I'm hurting you. I don't want to do that."

"I can hold you," Robbie insisted.

Lily stepped onto his back, pushed the tin roof panel up and tried to ease it to the side. The other end of the sheet squealed, and a nail scraped across wood. The panel moved and slid across the one next to it. Lily lowered it carefully, trying not to make any more noise than she already had.

Once she had the panel moved, she grabbed the edge of the wall and levered herself up until she balanced on her elbows and upper arms. From her perch, she could see the jungle less than three yards away from the shack. No one walked behind the building. To her left was a dilapidated tent barely standing upright, the canvas dingy with dirt and mildew.

Lily didn't see anyone around the side or back. But she could see men moving near the front. If they looked her way, they could possibly see her.

Knowing she might be seen at any time, she had to hurry. Lily slung her leg over the top of the wall and straddled it. Then she leaned back into the room and called out softly, "Robbie, can you lift Mari up to me?"

"Yes. I can." Robbie scrambled to his feet, grabbed Mari around the waist and lifted her as high as his little arms could reach. Lily stretched her arm as far as she could but couldn't quite reach the little girl.

"It's not high enough," Lily said.

"Wait. I know what to do." Robbie set Mari on the ground and knelt beside her. "Get on my shoulders, Mari, *por favor*."

Mari climbed up, holding onto Robbie's hair to steady herself. Then, bracing his hands on the wall, Robbie lurched to his feet and moved close enough Lily could reach out and snag Mari's hand. Clamping her thighs to each side of the wall, she hauled the little girl up to the top and sat for a moment until the muscles in her arms stopped hurting. Then she looked into Mari's eyes. "When I let go, you'll fall a little, but you'll be all right. Stay there. Don't leave until Robbie and I can go with you. Okay?"

Mari nodded. "*Estoy asustado*," she said, her eyes filling with tears.

Robbie spoke softly in Spanish.

Mari nodded.

"She's scared," Robbie said. "I told her she would be okay."

"Ready?" Lily asked.

Mari nodded again.

Holding onto Mari's wrists, Lily lowered her as much as she could and then let go, praying the child would land safely.

She held her breath until Mari pushed to her feet and grinned up at her.

Then Lily turned back to Robbie and reached down to help him up.

She stretched as much as she could but could barely touch the tips of Robbie's fingers. Her pulse raced. Already committed to this escape plan after dropping one child on the outside, she had to be able to get Robbie out as well. But he wasn't quite tall enough to reach her hand.

Desperate now, Lily leaned farther over the wall. She could still only touch his fingertips.

"Don't leave me, Miss Grayson," he whimpered, standing on his toes, reaching up as high as he could.

"Robbie, you're going to have to jump and grab my wrist with both hands."

Robbie nodded, his eyes brimming with tears.

"You can't cry, or you won't be able to see me to grab hold," Lily said softly. "You can do this."

Robbie scrubbed his hand across his eyes and nodded.

"Ready?" she whispered.

Before she could say jump, Robbie left the

ground, grabbed her wrist and held on with all his might.

Lily nearly fell back into the hut. Her legs strained to hold her at the top of the wall. For a moment, all she could do was hold on and pray. Then she leaned back, slowly sitting up, her back muscles screaming as she dragged Robbie up the side of the wall. When he could get his leg over the top, he let go of her hand and held on, breathing hard, his little body shaking.

Lily heard the sound of voices nearby and shot a glance toward the front of the building. Men walked down the middle of the camp, carrying rifles and what appeared to be military-grade weapons. Lily froze until they passed. Then she took Robbie's hand. "I'll let you down as far as I can then you'll drop to the ground."

He nodded.

Lily lowered him, her arms and back straining. When he was a low as she could manage, she released her hold.

The boy dropped to the ground and rolled up onto his feet.

Shouts rose up in the camp.

Lily cast one last glance toward the front of the shack and tents. Men were running toward the road leading into the encampment.

While their captors' attention was on something other than the prisoners in the shack, Lily dropped to the ground beside Mari and Robbie. She swung Mari up onto her back. "Hold on tight," she said.

Mari's little arms wrapped around her neck.

After a quick glance around her, Lily looked at Robbie. "Remember how fast you ran at recess?"

He nodded, his eyes wide

"I need you to run that fast again. But you have to stay with me."

He nodded and looked toward the jungle.

They left the shadows of the shack and raced for the jungle. Once they had pushed through bushes and brush and were deep enough into the gloom of the canopy, Lily slowed and turned back to see if they were being followed.

An explosion shook the ground beneath their feet, and gunfire erupted.

Lily dropped to the ground and took the children down with her. They'd gone deeply enough into the jungle that Lily could no longer see the camp, only hear the sounds of shouts and gunfire echoing off the hills.

Had Hank's team set the explosives? Were they there to rescue Lily and the kids?

If El Patron had discovered they were missing, he'd be angry. Were his men shooting indiscriminately toward the jungle, hoping to hit the missing captives?

Lily didn't want to risk the children being hit, so she stayed down, watched and waited for a few more minutes before she eased the children out of their hiding place and went deeper into the forest, farther away from the danger of being hit by a stray bullet. She prayed Tony, Hank and Marcus could find them before El Patron did.

The cartel leader would be angry enough, he wouldn't hesitate to kill.

CHAPTER 13

Tony had received the call on the satellite phone he'd brought with him, having forwarded his cellphone, knowing reception in some parts of Costa Rica could be nonexistent. When he'd heard Lily's voice, he'd clutched the phone in his hand so tightly, he'd thought he would crush it.

They were alive.

Based on the GPS tracker, they weren't too far away. Maybe five or six miles.

His team of operatives had turned off the narrow highway onto a dirt road that wound through the trees, heading deeper into the jungle toward the hills.

After El Patron ended the call, Tony leaned closer to Marcus's shoulder. "Can we go any faster?"

Marcus shook his head, his jaw tight, his knuckles white on the steering wheel as they bounced and jolted along the rutted road.

"When we get closer, we'll park the SUV in the bushes and go in on foot," Hank said.

Tony nodded.

"You might want to stay back with the vehicle," Hank suggested. "You're not trained in special operations combat."

"I'm going in." Tony held up a hand. "I'll hang back, so I don't sabotage the mission by doing something dumb, but I'm going in."

"You need to reconsider," Marcus said. "Those kids need their father alive."

"I can't stand back and wait for word. What if you're outnumbered?" Tony asked.

Hank's lips quirked. "We've been outnumbered before. We know how to get in quietly and take out as many as we can before they sound the alarm."

Tony's lips pressed into a thin line. "I know what you're saying. I might slow you down or give away your position. I won't do anything to risk the lives of Lily or my children. Again, I'll hang back and watch your backs."

"Hopefully, you won't shoot us in the back because you think we're one of them," Boomer said. "Even the best of us get confused in the chaos of battle."

"Look, I know how to handle a rifle or a pistol," Tony insisted. "I won't shoot unless I am one-hundred-percent certain it's not one of you, Lily or the kids."

Hank's mouth pressed into a grim line. "You'll stay back?"

Tony raised his hand as if swearing in at a court hearing. "I will."

"Give him a handgun," Hank called out.

Boomer reached over the back of the seat and pulled out a Glock nine-millimeter pistol and a box of bullets. He handed them over the back of Tony's seat. "Don't make us regret this."

Tony loaded the magazine and put extra bullets in his pockets.

When they were within a mile and a half of where the green dots had ceased moving, Marcus pulled the SUV off the dirt road and hid it behind several bushes.

The men climbed out, selected their choice of weapons and fitted radio communication earbuds in their ears, testing them before they headed out.

Hank gave Tony a set of the earbuds and showed him how to use them. Then he clapped him on the back and nodded to the team. "Let's do this."

They moved out swiftly, paralleling the road in case sentries had been posted to warn El Patron when their opposition arrived.

Tony was careful to move quietly through the trees. He watched as the others spread out, moving from shadow to shadow, keeping as low to the ground as they could, and still move out smartly.

Fifteen minutes later, they approached the location where the green lights on the GPS tracker still glowed brightly.

Hank waved Tony forward and showed him the device, and then pointed in the direction they were located. Then he pressed a finger to his lips and pointed to a place far to their right toward a clearing. A movement in the clearing made Tony freeze. A man stood with his back to a tree. He had a rifle slung over his shoulder and was smoking a cigarette.

Hank pointed to Taz and circled his finger toward the left.

Taz took off in a wide circle around the perimeter of the camp.

A few minutes later, a voice whispered into the headset in Tony's ear. "I count twelve bogeys that I can see. Three on perimeter, one by the road in, another thirty yards to his right the other thirty yards to his left. Nine in the camp. Four tents, a small hut, six vehicles and a barrel I assume contains fuel to run the vehicles."

"Any sign of the woman and children?" Hank asked softly.

"Negative," Taz replied.

Hank's eyes narrowed. "Can you create a diversion with that barrel of fuel?"

"I think so. The barrels on the edge of the camp. I can do even better than that; I can disable the vehicles while I'm at it. Nothing a little C4 won't stir up."

"Think diversion, not annihilation," Hank warned. "A little C4 goes a long way."

"Roger," Taz said.

"You sure the woman and kids are clear of the area you're about to fire up?" Hank asked.

"Clear," Taz responded.

"Notify us when you're ready," Hank said.

"Roger."

Hank handed Tony a miniature pair of binoculars. "Scan the camp and let me know when you locate El Patron. We don't want to go in guns a-blazin' if we're in the wrong place. While you're at it, let me know if you find Ms. Grayson and the kids."

Tony took them gladly, hoping he could find his family and get them out without one of them getting hit.

He trained the binoculars on the center of the camp and searched every face he saw for the one he would never forget. When he finally found him, his blood burned in his veins. "El Patron is there."

Hank nodded. "Either way, these people kidnapped a woman and two children. El Patron or not, they're going down." He turned to one of his men. "Boomer, swing around and get the guy on the far side. Make it quiet. Duke, take out the one on the road. Chuck, get the one nearest us."

"Sure, give the old guy the easy target. He's probably asleep," Chuck said.

"Be ready to move when the fireworks start," Hank said.

"Roger," came the response from Hank's four men.

A few minutes later, Taz's voice sounded across the radio, "Ready to rock and roll?"

"Roger," came the quiet responses from the others.

Hank pointed at Tony. "Stay here and watch for the stragglers deserting camp like rats off a sinking ship. Don't let them circle back and cause us problems. Remember, if you're firing toward camp, you run the risk of hitting one of us."

Tony nodded. "Roger."

Hank moved like a cat, hunkered low and inching stealthily toward the camp. He was halfway there, when an explosion destroyed the silence. A fireball shot up into the air as hundreds of gallons of fuel went up in flames. Two seconds later, another explosion shook the ground, then another and another. Tony counted seven all together. Six vehicles had been disabled. Along with the fuel they'd used to run them.

Gunfire erupted.

Tony ducked instinctively and peered through the binoculars toward the tent and hut. Men ran through camp first one direction and then the opposite. Chaos reigned. When they discovered they couldn't take the vehicles, because they'd been destroyed, they ran toward the road.

Swinging the binoculars around, he saw when Chuck, Duke and Boomer made their moves and took out the sentries. Then they moved in, sneaking up to a position where they could lay down fire and pick off the men one by one.

Tony had never shot a man in his life. He'd been instrumental in the capture of El Patron, but he hadn't had to kill anyone to make it happen. He knew if it came to saving the lives of people he loved, he'd sure as hell pull the trigger. Waiting and watching for escapees wasn't something he wanted to do but getting in the way of the trained professionals would only put himself, his family and the professionals at risk.

Tony stayed put and watched vigilantly.

After a while, a dark-haired, dark-skinned man with thick black brows ran out of the camp and straight toward Tony's position.

Tony lifted the binoculars and gasped. The man was El Patron. He raised his weapon and aimed for the man's chest. When it came time to pull the trigger, he couldn't. What if he missed? The bullet could travel as far as into the camp, where the Hank's team was rounding up bad guys. And he didn't know where they were keeping Lily and his children.

He waited until Patron was within easy range of the pistol, tracking El Patron with his hand gun. Still, he hesitated, not at all comfortable shooting in the direction where they might be keeping his family. His guess was that they were in one of the tents or the hut.

At that moment, one of the tents burst into flames.

Tony's attention shifted from the escaping Patron to the tent that had just burst into flame. "Hank, tell me my family wasn't in that tent."

"Not there yet," Hank replied.

Tony almost rose from his position, his heart in his throat, terrified his children and Lily were in that burning tent.

At that moment, El Patron ran past, a mere five yards away from where Tony lay.

Tony dropped his gun, leaped to his feet and ran after El Patron. He hit him from behind in a flying tackle and brought him down so hard, he knocked the wind out of the man.

El Patron bucked and rolled over, throwing Tony off him. He scrambled to his feet and pulled a knife out of a scabbard at his waist. "Now, you will pay for the two years I spent in prison." Patron snarled and lunged for Tony, swinging the knife at his gut.

Tony hopped backward, tripped over a branch and fell on his back.

El Patron dove after him, the knife coming down toward Tony's heart.

He caught the man's wrist in mid-air but strained to keep him from jabbing the blade into him.

They wrestled for control, rolling across the ground, grunting and straining.

Arms shaking with the effort, Tony twisted to the side and slammed El Patron's hand against a tree trunk.

The knife fell free of Patron's hand and dropped into the leaves.

When El Patron reached for it, Tony grabbed his arm and yanked it up between his shoulder blades, much as Lily had done to Michael's father in front of the schoolhouse. When the cartel leader tried to shake him off, Tony pushed his arm higher until the man was crying out in pain.

"Where are my children and the woman who was with them?" Tony demanded.

Patron snorted. "I killed them, like I killed *tu esposa*."

Deep red anger raged through Tony. If he'd had the gun in his hand, he would have put a bullet in the man's head. Instead, he pushed his arm up higher. If he broke it, he didn't care. The man was pure evil. "You lie," he said, praying he was right.

The drug lord laughed, his laughter cutting off as Tony pushed his arm up higher. "Go. You will see. *Están muertos*."

Hank's voice came through the headset in Tony's ear. "The camp is now under our control. Bring any prisoners in." He paused, and then continued. "Tony, they weren't in the tent or the hut. We haven't found Lily or your children."

Chuck approached Tony. "I'll take him," he said. "Go help the others find your family."

Tony waited until Chuck had El Patron's arm in his grip before he rose to his feet. He returned to where he'd left the handgun and picked it up from where he'd dropped it on the ground in his effort to capture El Patron.

When he turned back to Chuck, the older man had brought the cartel leader to his feet.

About to turn back toward the camp, Tony saw El Patron stumble and fall to the ground. The man reached out and grabbed the knife in the leaves, rolled over and stabbed at Chuck, hitting him in the calf.

Chuck reached for the man, but El Patron crab-walked out of Chuck's range.

El Patron rose to his feet and cocked his arm to swing again.

Tony raised the handgun, beyond tired, beyond fed up, and shot the drug lord in the chest.

El Patron's eyes widened. He dropped the knife, clutched his chest and looked toward Tony. Then he fell to his knees and toppled over, face-first on the ground.

"Are you all right, Chuck?" Tony asked.

He shook his head. "It's just a flesh wound. Go

find your family," he said as he ripped his shirt over his head and tied it around his calf.

With his nemesis down and Chuck capable of taking care of himself, Tony ran toward the camp, praying with each step he'd find Robbie, Mari and Lily alive and well. He'd hold his son, kiss his daughter and tell Lily he loved her.

Please, God, let me have that chance.

He found Hank in the middle of the camp, talking with Taz, Boomer, Duke and Marcus. When Tony approached, they all turned to face him.

Hank held out his hand, the GPS location device in his palm, no green dots glowing through a cracked screen. "I must have broken it when I fought with one of Patron's men." He shoved the device in his pocket and looked around. "We've gone through every tent and the hut and didn't find any sign that they've been here."

"We know they were," Tony said. "The beacons showed they were here."

"Perhaps they were taken out before we arrived," Marcus suggested.

Tony shook his head. This wasn't happening. They hadn't come this far for nothing. "We didn't see another vehicle leave. They wouldn't have taken them out on foot." Tony left the men and went through the tents still standing. He didn't know what he'd find, but he had to check for himself.

He found nothing.

When he ducked into the hut, he closed his eyes to let them adjust to the darkness. Was that the lingering scent of roses he could smell? He sniffed the air. Yes, it was the scent of roses. He opened his eyes and looked around at the empty space. A little bit of daylight shone down from the ceiling where a corrugated tin panel had been displaced, leaving a gap in the roof.

A gap large enough for a small woman to get through.

Tony laughed and ran out of the building.

"What did you find?"

"Nothing. Absolutely nothing," he said as he rounded the building and ran to the back. There in the dirt, he found three sets of footprints.

Marcus ran up behind him.

Tony turned to his friend and grabbed his arms. "She got them out. Lily got them out!" He turned and ran into the jungle. "Lily! Robbie! Mari!"

The others who weren't guarding prisoners joined them, spreading out in a line, all calling out as they moved through the trees, bushes and vines.

Tony's excitement began to fade as they moved deeper into the jungle. They had to be out there. "Lily! Robbie! Mari!"

Then he heard it, the sound that made his heart sing.

"Tony?" came a wavering cry.

"Lily! Where are you?"

"Papi," Robbie's voice sounded in the shadows.

Lily appeared in the distance, weaving through the vines and brush, Mari in her arms and Robbie at her side.

Tony ran to them, calling out, "I found them," to the others still on their headsets.

When he reached them, he wrapped his arms around all three and held them until his heartbeat slowed and he could talk past the lump in his throat. "He told me he'd killed you," Tony whispered in Lily's ear.

"El Patron?" Lily looked past him toward the camp, her brow furrowing. "Did you catch him?"

"He won't bother us ever again," Tony said.

Lily captured his gaze. "Is he…?"

Tony nodded. "Dead."

Lily wrapped her free arm around his neck and hugged him tight. "Thank God," she said. "Thank God."

Tony kissed her cheek, her eyes, her lips and then kissed Mari's cheek and the top of Robbie's head. "I've never been happier to see anyone in my life." He bent and picked up Robbie then turned with Lily and Mari to head back to the camp,

Hank, Marcus, Boomer, Taz, Duke and Chuck gathered around them, all expressing their relief that they were all okay and their amazement that Lily had managed to get the kids out of the hut and hidden in the jungle.

Marcus hiked back to get the SUV, while Tony used his satellite phone to call the authorities to come collect the remaining members of El Patron's drug ring.

Hank, Marcus, Boomer and Taz remained behind to guard the prisoners until the authorities could get there and to answer their questions.

Duke loaded the weapons into the SUV and helped Chuck into the front passenger seat, while Tony settled Robbie and Mari in the back row of seats and helped Lily up into the middle seats. He slid in beside her and closed the door, a euphoric sense of relief washing over him.

In the back seat, Mari fell asleep on the way back. Robbie yawned and rubbed his eyes. "If the bad guys aren't going to bother us anymore, does that mean we can stay and go fishing again?" His voice faded as he closed his eyes.

"If you want to stay the rest of the summer, you can," Tony said.

Robbie opened his eyes and smiled. "I want to catch a bigger fish."

"I guess that means you want to stay."

Robbie nodded and closed his eyes, a smile on his face.

Tony turned to Lily. "I'll completely understand if you want to go back to Texas, after all that's happened."

She reached for his hand. "I want to stay with you, if you want me to."

He lifted her hand to his lips. "I want that more than you can ever know. Please, stay."

She nodded. "I can't think of anywhere I'd rather be." Lily leaned against his shoulder, and they held hands all the way back to the hotel.

Once there, they all showered and changed into nice clothes and went down to dinner.

Marcus, Hank and the rest of the Brotherhood Protectors team arrived halfway through the meal and joined them. Afterward, Tony took his family to the nightclub where they danced until Mari laid down in the middle of the dance floor and fell asleep.

They said their goodnights to the men who'd helped rescue them and retired to the penthouse where Tony and Lily tucked in two very tired, but happy children, kissing them both goodnight.

Robbie looked up at Lily, his eyes drooping heavily. "Are you going to marry my Papi?"

Lily smiled down at Robbie. "I don't know, Robbie."

Tony stepped up behind Lily and slid an arm around her waist. "Would you like that?"

Robbie nodded his head. "Then I wouldn't have to call her Miss Grayson or Auntie Lily." He yawned and turned on his side. "I'd call her mama."

Lily shot a glance at Tony.

He pressed a finger to her lips, took her hand and led her out of the room.

Once they were in the living room, she turned toward him. "I didn't prompt him to say that. I know how much you loved your wife, and I'd never presume to take her place."

Again, Tony pressed a finger to her mouth. Then he replaced it with his lips. "I loved Marisol with all my heart. She was a dear wife and a good mother."

Lily nodded, her eyes filling with tears. "I'm so sorry you lost her."

"I am too." Tony stared down into her eyes. "But she would have wanted me to keep on living, to fall in love and help my children grow and mature in the best manner possible. She'd want me to remarry. And she'd have wanted her children to have whoever I chose to love her children as much as she did."

"I love Robbie and Mari," Lily said.

Tony smiled. "You've proven that again and again. You've even risked your own life to save theirs. And you straightened me out when I fell down on the job of being a good father to them."

"I only did what I thought was right." She sighed. "I can be bossy."

"In a good way," he said and pressed a kiss to the tip of her nose.

"So, where do we go from here?" she asked.

"I know what I want," Tony said. "But we've only

known each other for a short time. I want to give you more time to know what you want."

She wrapped her arms around his neck and pressed her body against his. "I don't need more time. When I know what I want, I don't wait to make up my mind." She looked up at him, her eyes shining and her cheeks glowing. "I want you."

"I want you more." Tony swept her up in his arms, carried her to his bedroom, and closed the door.

CHAPTER 14

Two months later...

"Are you ready for school to start tomorrow?" Nash asked as he sat on the porch swing at the Grayson Ranch with Phoebe, his finance, beside him.

Lily leaned her back against Tony's chest, a smile on her face and warmth swelling her heart. "I'm ready. Robbie and Mari helped me decorate my room with some of the things we brought back from Costa Rica. We even hung the pictures we had blown up of the yellowfin tuna Robbie caught that was bigger than him. He was so proud of that fish."

Robbie and Mari played in the yard with a beach ball they'd brought back from their summer in Manuel Antonio.

"Any recurring nightmares from their ordeal with

the drug cartel?" Kinsey asked. She sat in Beckett's lap, in one of the half dozen rocking chairs that lined the porch.

Lily shook her head. "After the first week, they were fine. Knowing El Patron couldn't come after them, ever again, seemed to help. They look forward to spending part of the Christmas vacation there and every summer." She chuckled. "Robbie wants to be a boat captain like Marcus when he grows up, and Mari wants to be a mermaid."

"Have you two set a wedding date?" Lola asked. She and Daniel manned the grill, cooking the steaks and chicken breasts for the last family gathering before summer officially ended, and the school year began

"Well…actually," Lily smiled slyly and turned to Tony. "You want to tell them?"

Tony chuckled. "I don't want to get shot at my first Grayson family gathering. Maybe it would be better coming from you." He kissed her lips and raised his eyebrows.

"Coward," she muttered then reached into her pocket and pulled out her rings and slipped them onto her left hand. Then she held up her hand for all to see, a grin spreading across her face. "Tony and I couldn't wait. We got married in Costa Rica a week ago yesterday. You're looking at Mr. and Mrs. Antonio Delossantos."

Through all the congratulations and well wishes,

the steaks were overcooked, and the chicken turned to rubber.

Lily didn't care. She had her family around her, and the loves of her life were now a part of that family. She hadn't thought life could be any better, but it could, as she'd learned that morning in the bathroom.

"And just so you know, not only am I now a married woman, Tony, Robbie, Mari and I are expecting a baby next spring."

Tony's eyes widened, and his jaw dropped before snapping shut again. "Are you serious?"

"You didn't tell him first?" Her brother Rider shook his head. "That's pretty low. If my woman was pregnant, I'd want to be the first to know."

His fiancé, Salina, leaned close to him and whispered into his ear.

"What?" Rider exclaimed. "You are?"

"I wanted to surprise you tonight," she grinned. "But I couldn't wait. We're going to have a baby next spring as well." She patted her belly. "Thank goodness I'll graduate from PA school in December."

"That means we have a wedding to plan for Salina and Rider between now and then," Kinsey said and gave a teasing glare toward Lily and Tony. "Since the baby of the family didn't give us the chance to make a fuss over her nuptials."

After all the hugs made their rounds, Lily settled on the porch steps beside Tony and slipped her arm through his. "Think Robbie and Mari will be all right having a little brother or sister?"

"I know they will. Robbie is already so good with Mari. He'll be a natural with a little brother."

"Or another little sister," Lily said.

"And Mari will love that she won't be the littlest member of the family. She already thinks she's big stuff since she's starting kindergarten this fall."

"And to think," Tony said. "This all started because a feisty teacher impressed a crusty old grouch with her Krav Maga skills enough to hire her to protect his children."

"Don't be so flippant," Lily said. "Robbie is getting really good at some of the moves I've been teaching him. And Mari's going to be a real ball buster."

"Good," Tony said. "I don't want any man taking advantage of my little girl."

A pager buzzed. Then another and another. Lily's brothers and Daniel all looked down at the ones they carried.

"Guess our steaks are going to have to wait." Beckett kissed Kinsey and took off toward his truck.

"Duty calls. Joe Sarly's barn is on fire," Chance said and chucked his girl, Kate, beneath the chin. "See ya, darlin'."

She snorted. "You're not leaving without me and Bacchus." She whistled and Bacchus, her trained Belgian Malinois, came running. They left in Chance's truck, followed by Nash, Rider and Daniel.

Lily cocked an eyebrow toward her husband. "I suppose you'll be joining the volunteer firefighters next."

He nodded. "I've been thinking about it."

"I was considering it myself," Lily said. "Until I discovered I'm pregnant."

"I guess your service to the county will have to wait until after we have our baby." Tony hugged her tight, grinning. "We're having a baby."

Lily's heart swelled with all the love she had for the man she'd married. "I love you, Mr. Delossantos."

"I love you more, Mrs. Delossantos."

SOLDIER'S DUTY

IRON HORSE LEGACY BOOK #1

Elle James
New York Times Bestselling Author

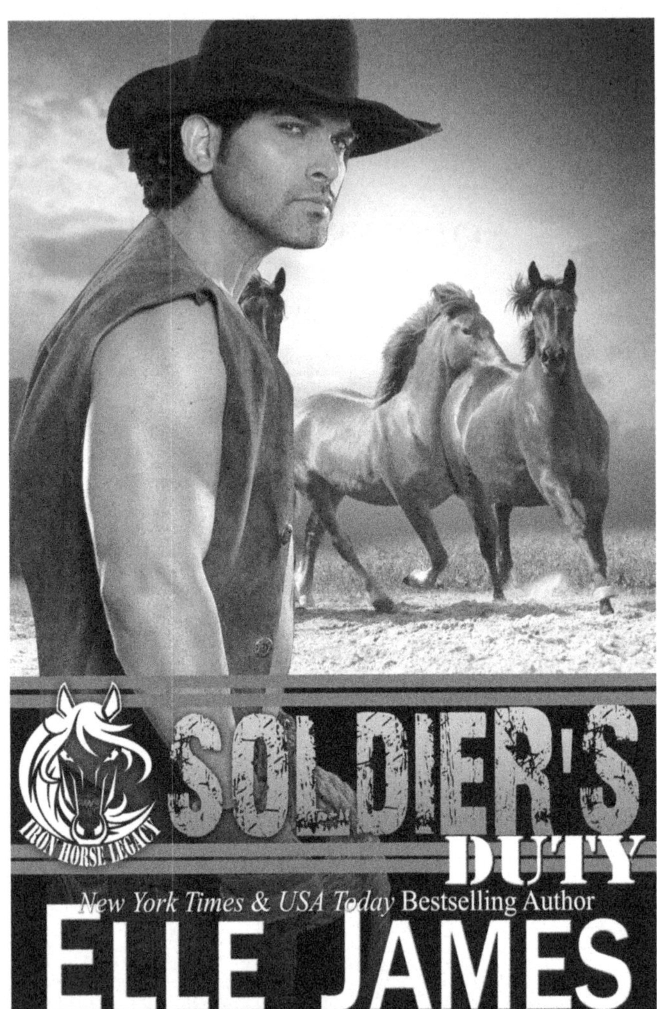
IRON HORSE LEGACY
SOLDIER'S
DUTY
New York Times & USA Today Bestselling Author
ELLE JAMES

CHAPTER 1

"As you all know, William Reed escaped from a prison transport yesterday." Sheriff Barron stood in front of a group of men and women who'd gathered around him at the side of the highway in the foothills of the Crazy Mountains on a blustery cold day in early April.

He continued, "We have security camera footage showing him stealing a car from a convenience store in Bozeman. The license plate of the vehicle he stole matches the license plate of the vehicle behind me." Sheriff Barron turned to the side and waved toward a vehicle half-hidden in the brush behind him. "The state police are on their way, and they're also sending a helicopter from Bozeman. But they aren't as familiar with the mountainous terrain as you are, and the weather might keep them from using the chopper. That's why I've asked you to bring your horses and ATVs. All of you know these mountains better than anyone. And you are the select group of people I trust most to handle this situation."

James McKinnon tugged up the collar of his coat around his chin to keep a blast of wintery wind from snaking down his neck. He listened silently as the sheriff explained why they were there. With each breath James took, he blew out a little cloud of steam.

Rucker, his bay gelding, pawed at the ground impatiently.

James had chosen Rucker because he was the most sure-footed of the horses in his stable. For the manhunt they were about to conduct, the gelding was the best bet. The Crazy Mountains could be as dangerous as the man they were searching for. And the weather wasn't helping.

The sheriff gave them a steely glance. "We don't know at this point whether or not Reed is armed but assume that he is."

James's hand went to the pistol in the holster he had strapped to his hip.

"Sheriff, what do you want us to do?" one of the men in the crowd called out.

The sheriff straightened, with his shoulders pushed back and his mouth set in a firm line. He stared at each of the people gathered around, making eye contact with each person. "Bring him in."

"And how do you want us to do that," another man called out.

The sheriff's chin lifted. "Most of you follow the news. Reed was in prison for multiple counts of murder. He killed two guards during the armored truck robbery. When he was cornered, he killed two cops. The man was serving a life sentence without parole.

"While being transported to a high-security prison, his transport vehicle ran off the road. The driver was killed on impact, but the guard in back with Reed wasn't. He was injured. Reed finished him off. Now, I'm not telling you to kill Reed, but if at any time believe your life is in danger, shoot to kill the bastard. If at all possible, don't engage…report. Our primary goal is to bring Reed in before he hurts anyone else."

James's hands tightened into fists. He hadn't killed a man since he'd been a member of Delta Force more than two decades ago. Not that he'd become squeamish about killing a man in his old age, but it was just that he'd thought his people-killing days were over when he'd left the military.

The only killing he'd done lately was the occasional coyote in the chicken coop and deer or elk while hunting in the fall.

From the news reports he'd been following, he knew Reed had turned into a really bad character.

James was glad the bastard had headed into the mountains instead of the city. He reckoned that if the convict was cornered, he would take whatever hostage he could to get out of a situation.

James had left instructions with his wife and daughter to stay inside the ranch house and keep the doors locked. But he knew they were stubborn women and wouldn't stand by and leave the animals to fend for themselves, especially in bad weather. They'd venture out into the barnyard to feed the chickens, pigs, horses and goats to keep them from going hungry. With the winter weather making a reappearance, they'd likely put some of the livestock in the barn.

Which would leave them at risk of being captured if Reed circled back to the Iron Horse Ranch. Hopefully, they'd be smart and enlist the help of their ranch foreman, Parker Bailey.

Sheriff Barron held up a paper with an image of William Reed. James didn't need to see the picture. He knew Reed. However, others amongst them were newer to Eagle Rock and the county. "This is our man. Right now, we think he's up in the mountains. The longer he's free, the hungrier he'll get. It's imperative we bring him in quickly. All of our families' lives are in danger as long as he runs free."

"Then let's stop talking and start tracking," Marty Langley called out.

The sheriff nodded. "All right, then, gather

around the map. We're going to split up into different quadrants so we're not shooting at each other." Sheriff Barron spread a map over the hood of his SUV, and the group gathered around him. He gave instructions as to where each person would be during the hunt and what signal they should give if they found something. He handed out as many two-way radios as he had, distributing them to every other quadrant.

Once James had his assigned area, he mounted Rucker and rode into the mountains, his knee nudging the rifle in his scabbard, his hand patting the pistol on his hip.

He'd known Reed for years. When you lived in a small community, everyone knew everyone else. Some were better at keeping secrets than others but, for the most part, everyone knew everyone else's business.

Reed had been a regular guy, working in construction and hitting the bar at night. He'd been a ladies' man with a lot going for him. How had a guy like that ended up robbing an armored truck and killing the people driving it? What had driven Reed down the wrong path?

James could have been home with his wife of thirty-five wonderful years, holding her close in front of the fireplace, instead of riding out on a cold winter's night in search of a killer.

He knew he had it good. After twenty years in the

military, he'd settled in Montana on the land his father had passed down to him. He'd wanted his kids to have what he'd had growing up. Ranching had made him the man he was—unafraid of hard work, determined to make a difference, able to take on any challenge, no matter how physically or mentally difficult.

He'd been damned proud of his sons and daughter and how they'd taken to ranching like they'd been born to it. Even Angus, who'd been twelve when they'd moved to the Crazy Mountains of Montana. He'd been the first to learn to ride and show the other boys how wonderful it could be to have the wind in their faces, galloping across the pastures.

A cold wind whipped into James's face, bringing him back to the present and the bitterness of an early spring cold snap. Just when they'd thought spring had come and the snow had started to melt at the lower elevations, the jet stream had taken a violent shift downward, dipping south from Canada into the Rocky Mountains of Montana, dumping a foot of fresh snow all the way down into the valleys.

He nudged Rucker in the flanks, sending him up the path leading to a small canyon that crossed over a couple of ranches—including his, the Iron Horse Ranch.

He knew the area better than anyone, having lived

on the ranch as a child and as an adult since he'd returned from serving in the Army. As his father's only child, he'd inherited the ranch upon his father's death. Now, it was up to him to make it sustainable and safe for his family and ranch hands.

Again, he thought about his wife, Hannah, and his daughter, Molly, and worried for their safety.

Clouds sank low over the mountaintops, bringing with it more snow, falling in giant flakes. The wind drove them sideways, making it difficult to see the trail ahead.

About the time James decided to turn back, he'd entered the canyon. Sheer walls of rock blocked some of the wind and snow, making it a little easier to see the path in front of Rucker.

James decided to give the hunt a little more time before he gave up and returned to the highway where he'd parked his horse trailer.

He knew of several caves in the canyon suitable for a fugitive to hole up in during a brutal winter storm. They weren't much further along the trail, but they were higher up the slope. Snowcapped ridges rose up beside him. He was careful not to make any loud noises that might trigger an avalanche. Spending the next couple days in a cave wasn't something he wanted to do.

If he survived an avalanche, he could make do with the natural shelter until a rescue chopper could get into the canyon and fish him out. But Hannah and Molly would be sick with worry. James tried not to put himself in situations that made his sweet wife worry. Unfortunately, the Reed escape had worry written all over it. The man had escaped. He'd already proven he'd kill rather than go back to jail. He wouldn't go peacefully.

Rucker climbed higher up the side of the canyon wall, following a narrow path dusted in snow. The wind blew the majority of the flakes away, keeping the rocky ground fairly recognizable.

The trail had been there for as long as James could remember. His father had told him it was a trail created by the Native Americans who'd once used the caves for shelter over a century ago.

Rucker stumbled on a rock and lurched to the side.

James's heart skipped several beats as he held onto the saddle horn.

Once Rucker regained his balance, he continued up the slope, plodding along, the snow pelting his eyes. He shook his head and whinnied softly.

James patted the horse's neck. "It's okay. Only a little farther, and we'll head back to the barn." The weather in early April was unpredictable. It could stop snowing altogether or become a white-out blizzard in a matter of minutes.

The first in the row of caves James remembered

appeared ahead and up the slope to his left. He dropped down from his horse's back and studied the dark opening. If he recalled correctly, the cave was little more than five or six feet back into the mountain side. Not enough to protect a man from the cold wind and driving snow.

James grabbed Rucker's reins and moved on to the next cave, glancing up the side of the hill as he approached.

The hackles on the back of his neck rose to attention. Had he seen movement in the shadowy entrance?

He stopped beside a small tree growing out of the side of the hill and looped Rucker's reins loosely over a branch. The horse wouldn't attempt to pull free. Rucker knew to hold fast. A loud noise might scare him into bolting for the barn. Otherwise, he'd stay put until James returned.

Pulling his handgun from the holster, James started up the incline toward the cave, his focus on the entrance and the overhang of snow on the slope above the cave. With the recent melting and the added layer of fresh snow, the snow above the cave could easily become unstable. Anything, including a gust of wind, could trigger an avalanche, sending snow and rocks crashing down the hillside.

James hoped he'd left Rucker well out of the path of the potential avalanche. If the snow started down the side of the hill, James would be forced to run for the cave and take shelter there. Possibly with a killer.

More reason to get up to the cave, check it out and get back down to Rucker as soon as possible. He should have turned back when the snow got so thick he could barely see the trail. If one of his sons or daughter had continued on, he would have reamed them for their irresponsible behavior. And here he was doing what he would expect them to avoid.

However, since he was there, he would check the cave. Then he'd head straight back to the highway and home. The search for the fugitive could continue the next day, after the snowstorm ended. Reed wouldn't make much headway in the current weather, anyway.

With his plan in mind, James trudged up the hill to the cave. He had camped in this particular grotto one fall when he'd been caught in a storm while out hunting elk. It went back far enough into the mountain to protect him from the wind and rain and was open enough to allow him to build a fire. He'd even staged additional firewood in case he ever got caught in a storm again. Then at least, he'd have dry wood to build a warming fire.

If Reed was up in this canyon, this cave would be the perfect shelter from the current storm. The next one in line was harder to find and had a narrower entrance.

As he neared the mouth of the cavern, he drew on

his Delta Force training, treading lightly and keeping as much of his body out of direct line of fire as possible as he edged around the corner and peered into the shadows.

The sound of voices echoed softly from the darkness near the back of the cave. He smelled wood smoke before he spotted the yellow glow of a fire, shedding light on two figures standing nearby.

"Where is it?" one voice was saying, the tone urgent, strained.

"I'm not telling you. If I tell you, you have no reason to keep me alive."

James stiffened. He remembered having a conversation with Reed outside the hardware store in Eagle Rock several years ago. That husky, deep voice wasn't something a person forgot.

His pulse quickening, James knew he had to get back down the mountain to the sheriff and let him know what he'd found. They weren't supposed to engage, just report.

But he hadn't expected to find Reed with someone else. If he left and reported to the sheriff without identifying the other man and the two men managed to get out of the canyon before they were captured by the authorities, no one would know who was helping Reed.

"I got you out of there, the least you can do is share your secret."

"I put it somewhere no one will find it. If I die, it

goes to the grave with me," Reed said. "I did that on purpose. I can't trust anyone. If you want to know where it is, you'll have to get me out of Montana alive."

"I told you I would. You have my word. But you can't leave Montana without it."

"No, but I can leave Montana without you. If I've learned one thing in prison," Reed's voice grew deeper, "the only person you can trust is yourself."

"Damn it, Reed, we don't have time to dick around. Sheriff Barron has a posse combing the mountains. The only thing keeping them from finding you is the storm moving in. Get the money, and let's get the hell out of here."

James strained to see into the darkness, but the man with Reed had his back to the cave entrance and appeared to be wearing a knit ski hat. The voice was familiar, but he couldn't put his finger on who it was. He leaned into the cave a little more, waiting for the man to shift into a position where the fire would light up his face.

"You know, there's a bounty on your head," the man told Reed, in a threatening tone. "Maybe I don't want your bag of money. It's probably marked anyway. I could turn you in and collect the reward. I'd have the money and be a hero for saving the world from a killer."

Reed lunged toward the other man, knocking him back, his face even deeper in the shadows, or was it covered in a ski mask? "You dare threaten me?" He lifted the man off his feet and shoved him against the wall. "Do you know the hell I've lived in for the past thirteen years? I've seen men like you who've had their tongues carved out with a spoon. I didn't get out of prison to put up with the likes of you."

The man being held against the wall gagged, his feet scraping against the hard rock surface behind him.

James couldn't let Reed kill the other man, even if the other man happened to be the one who'd helped him escape from prison. Taking a deep breath, he called out, "Drop him, Reed, or I'll shoot."

The convict froze with his hand still gripping the other man's throat. "Guess you're gonna have to shoot." Then he spun, dragging his captive with him, and using his body as a shield.

Since his back was still to James, James couldn't see who it was.

"Go ahead," Reed taunted. "Shoot. This piece of shit deserves to die."

The man he held fumbled in his jacket pocket, pulled out something long and shiny and then shoved it toward Reed.

Reed gasped, his eyes widening. "Bastard," he said, his voice more of a wheeze. His grip loosened on his captive.

The man slumped to his knees and bent over.

Reed stood for a long moment, his hand curling

around the knife protruding from his chest. He gripped the handle and pulled it out. He stared at it, and then at James, and collapsed on top of the man he'd almost killed.

James rushed forward, jammed his handgun into his holster and felt for a pulse in Reed's neck. He had one, but it was faint and fluttering erratically.

The man beneath him, grunted and pushed at the bulk of the dead man weighing him down. "Help me," he said.

James grabbed Reed's arm and pulled him off the other man, laying him flat on his back.

Reed stared up at James, his eyes narrowing. He whispered something.

James leaned close, barely able to hear.

"Where the…snake…threads…needle's eye," Reed coughed, and blood dribbled out of the side of his mouth.

James pressed his hand to the wound in Reed's chest. Having seen similar wounds in Iraq, he figured the knife had damaged a major organ, and Reed wasn't going to make it out of that cave alive.

Reed raised a hand and clutched his collar in a surprisingly strong grip. "They'll never find it." He chuckled, a gurgling sound that caused more blood to ooze from the corner of his mouth. Then his hand dropped to his side, and his body went limp.

James pressed two fingers to the base of Reed's

throat, feeling for a pulse. When he felt none, he started to straighten.

Something cold and hard pressed to his temple. "Move, and I'll shoot."

His heart hammering against his ribs, James reached for the gun at his side. A cold feeling washed over him that had nothing to do with the gale-force winds blasting down through the canyon outside the walls of the cave.

His holster was empty. He couldn't believe he'd helped the other man, only to have him take his gun and turn it on him.

"What did Reed say before he died?" the man behind him demanded.

James held up his hands, shaking his head. "I don't remember."

"You better start, or you can join him in his cold place in hell."

"Seriously, I couldn't hear what he said. It was all garbled."

"He said something about a needle. I know you heard him. Tell me." The angry guy behind him fired the gun, hitting James in the right arm.

Pain knifed through his arm, and it hung limp against his side.

"Tell me, or I'll shoot again."

Outside, a rumbling sound made James forget about being shot at again. "If you want to get out of this cave alive, we have to leave now."

"I'm the one with the gun. I say when we leave."

"Then you'll have to shoot me, because I'm not going to be trapped in this cave by an avalanche." James lurched to his feet and started for the entrance.

Rocks and snow started to fall from the slope above the cave's entrance.

"Avalanche," James called out.

The entire hillside to the south of the cave seemed to be slipping downward toward the floor of the canyon.

"Stop, or I'll shoot again!" the man in the ski mask yelled.

"That's what got the avalanche started in the first place. If you shoot again, even more will come crashing down on us." James kept moving toward the cave entrance, looking north at a narrow trail leading out of the other side of the cave from where he'd entered. "If you want to live, you better follow me, and for the love of God, don't shoot again." He'd figure another way out of this mess, if he didn't bleed out first. For now, James knew he had to get the hell out of there. If they stayed inside the cave, they'd be trapped. If they hurried out the north end, they might make it away from the avalanche.

Rocks and snow pelted his back as he hurried across the slippery slope, praying the bulk of the avalanche was well on its way to the south. But more snow and rocks rushed toward him and the man holding a gun on him. His head light from blood loss,

James ran, stumbling and skidding across loose gravel and tripping over small boulders. A rush of snow and debris scooped his feet out from under him and sent him sliding down the slope. He fought to keep his head above the snow. Then he crashed into something hard and everything went black.

ABOUT THE AUTHOR

ELLE JAMES also writing as MYLA JACKSON is a *New York Times* and *USA Today* Bestselling author of books including cowboys, intrigues and paranormal adventures that keep her readers on the edges of their seats. When she's not at her computer, she's traveling, snow skiing, boating, or riding her ATV, dreaming up new stories. Learn more about Elle James at www.ellejames.com

Website | Facebook | Twitter | GoodReads |
Newsletter | BookBub | Amazon

Or visit her alter ego Myla Jackson at
mylajackson.com
Website | Facebook | Twitter | Newsletter

Follow Me!
www.ellejames.com
ellejames@ellejames.com

ALSO BY ELLE JAMES

Iron Horse Legacy Series

Soldier's Duty (#1)

Ranger's Baby (#2)

Marine's Promise (#3) TBD

SEAL's Vow (#4) TBD

Brotherhood Protectors Series

Montana SEAL (#1)

Bride Protector SEAL (#2)

Montana D-Force (#3)

Cowboy D-Force (#4)

Montana Ranger (#5)

Montana Dog Soldier (#6)

Montana SEAL Daddy (#7)

Montana Ranger's Wedding Vow (#8)

Montana SEAL Undercover Daddy (#9)

Cape Cod SEAL Rescue (#10)

Montana SEAL Friendly Fire (#11)

Montana SEAL's Bride (#12)

Montana Rescue (Sleeper SEAL)

Hot SEAL Salty Dog (SEALs in Paradise)

Brotherhood Protectors Vol 1

Hellfire Series

Hellfire, Texas (#1)

Justice Burning (#2)

Smoldering Desire (#3)

Hellfire in High Heels (#4)

Playing With Fire (#5)

Up in Flames (#6)

Total Meltdown (#7)

Declan's Defenders

Marine Force Recon (#1)

Show of Force (#2)

Full Force (#3)

Driving Force (#4)

Mission: Six

One Intrepid SEAL

Two Dauntless Hearts

Three Courageous Words

Four Relentless Days

Five Ways to Surrender

Six Minutes to Midnight

Hearts & Heroes Series

Wyatt's War (#1)

Mack's Witness (#2)

Ronin's Return (#3)

Sam's Surrender (#4)

Take No Prisoners Series

SEAL's Honor (#1)

SEAL'S Desire (#2)

SEAL's Embrace (#3)

SEAL's Obsession (#4)

SEAL's Proposal (#5)

SEAL's Seduction (#6)

SEAL'S Defiance (#7)

SEAL's Deception (#8)

SEAL's Deliverance (#9)

SEAL's Ultimate Challenge (#10)

Texas Billionaire Club

Tarzan & Janine (#1)

Something To Talk About (#2)

Who's Your Daddy (#3)

Love & War (#4)

Ballistic Cowboy

Hot Combat (#1)

Hot Target (#2)

Hot Zone (#3)

Hot Velocity (#4)

Cajun Magic Mystery Series

Voodoo on the Bayou (#1)

Voodoo for Two (#2)

Deja Voodoo (#3)

Cajun Magic Mysteries Books 1-3

Billionaire Online Dating Service

The Billionaire Husband Test (#1)

The Billionaire Cinderella Test (#2)

The Billionaire Bride Test (#3)

The Billionaire Matchmaker Test (#4)

SEAL Of My Own

Navy SEAL Survival

Navy SEAL Captive

Navy SEAL To Die For

Navy SEAL Six Pack

Made in the USA
Las Vegas, NV
13 October 2021

32285745R00125